Out of the Darkness

Ray was wondering just how much trouble they were going to be in, when an ear-piercing blare shattered the stillness. He looked up and began to scream. A monstrous creature with curved fangs, flashing red eyes, and a face that made sudden death seem like a pleasant alternative was heading straight for him. Its clawlike hands were stretching and grasping ahead of it.

"Run!" screamed Ray.

Trip didn't need any encouragement. He sprinted to his right like a rabbit startled by a hound.

BRUCE COVILLE

THE A.I. GANG

ROBOT TROUBLE

A MINSTREL® BOOK

PUBLISHED BY POCKET BOOKS

New York   London   Toronto   Sydney   Tokyo   Singapore

A Minstrel Book published by
POCKET BOOKS, a division of Simon & Schuster Inc.
1230 Avenue of the Americas, New York, NY 10020

Copyright © 1986, 1995 by Bruce Coville

ISBN: 0-671-89252-5

First Minstrel Books printing April 1995

10 9 8 7 6 5 4 3 2 1

A MINSTREL BOOK and colophon are registered trademarks of Simon & Schuster Inc.

Cover art by Broeck Steadman

Printed in the U.S.A.

To my mother, who gave me the gift of music.

1

Two Spies

THIS ENTIRE MESS IS THE FAULT OF THOSE BRATS WHO call themselves the A.I. Gang! thought the shadowy figure slipping into the secret room hidden beneath the Anza-bora Island computer center. *If they had minded their own business, everything would be fine.*

The figure crossed to the far side of the room and thrust a pair of black-gloved hands into a cage mounted on the wall. The birds inside began to flutter and scuffle. After a moment the hands closed over one of them and drew it from the cage.

"This is insane!" muttered the mysterious figure, deftly strapping a capsule to the bird's leg. "I'm on an island equipped with the most advanced technology in the world. Yet to communicate with my Executive Council, I am forced to resort to the most primitive methods imaginable. If those A.I. brats don't watch out—"

The words were interrupted by a soft cooing. The black-gloved figure glanced at the pigeon, then laughed. It was only a bird. How could it know that the person holding it was Black Glove, chief operative of G.H.O.S.T.? Or that G.H.O.S.T. was trying to steal the secrets of the world's most advanced computer project? Or that those secrets were guarded by an electronic blanket that shielded Anza-bora Island from the outside world—a blanket that could have been pierced by the transmitter Black Glove had mounted inside the Project Alpha computer, if those kids hadn't found and removed it!

No, the pigeon only knew that it wanted to be free to fly home.

Black Glove wrapped the bird in a towel, then stuffed the towel into a gym bag. It was late and the computer center should be empty. Still, there was no point in taking any chances.

On the next floor up the spy spotted a light in an open office—one of the Project Alpha scientists working late. Quickly the black gloves were stripped off and hidden in the pocket of a white lab coat.

The researcher glanced up from her work and nodded pleasantly as Black Glove passed her doorway. And why not? In day-to-day life Black Glove was a well-known island personality. No one suspected that the friendly smile they knew so well masked a deadly, now desperate, enemy.

Outside the computer center the spy unwrapped the pigeon. A moment later the bird was soaring toward the clouds. Cutting an arc across the sky, it headed east, toward home—G.H.O.S.T. headquarters.

Black Glove felt an uncomfortable shiver. The Executive Council of G.H.O.S.T. could be most unpleasant when it was angry. And it was sure to be angry when it got the message the pigeon carried:

Transmission of data delayed by unexpected circumstances. Seeking new route to get information off island.   B.G.

Black Glove faded into the shadows, thinking furiously. There had to be some other way to get information off Anza-bora, a way those nosy kids couldn't interfere with.

Of course, the fact that the kids thought their enemy had fled the island on a stolen boat should help slow them down. But even so. . . .

Reentering the computer center, Black Glove vowed two things. First, there would be no rest until the new information path was established. Second, this time no one would be allowed to stand in the way.

Not even the A.I. Gang.

Not even if they were just kids.

Not even if that meant it would cost them their lives.

Heading back to the secret room, the spy patted the pockets of the white lab coat, then shivered with a wave of cold terror.

One glove was missing. . . .

Ramon Korbuscek moved slowly toward the abandoned building. It was a windmill, ruined by one or another of Central Europe's seemingly endless wars.

Someone with extremely good eyes *might* have been able to see him picking his way through the shadows that surrounded the windmill—but probably not. Nor would they have heard him, for Korbuscek moved as silently as a hawk floating on the wind.

Associated with no government, loyal to no single organization, he was one of the deadliest free agents in the world.

He paused to study his destination. One crumpled blade rested on the ground. The others, battered and torn by time, weather, and war, cast eerie, broken shadows around him.

A moment later the spy slipped beneath the crumpled blade. He whistled a five-note tune as he entered the building. A pair of rats scurried away from his feet. Pigeons cooed and whirred above him.

All else was silent.

Korbuscek frowned and whistled again.

From the darkest shadows on the opposite side of the mill came an answering whistle—not the same tune, but a variant of it, chosen months earlier as a signal for this meeting.

Korbuscek moved slowly across the floor, careful to avoid the gaping holes, many of them large enough to drop him through to the basement.

A woman emerged from the shadows. "I have your orders." Her voice was low and husky. Her hand trembled as she held out a brown envelope.

"And my money?"

The woman frowned. She was well aware of how much Korbuscek would make for this job, and she considered the fee outrageous. But her superiors decided these matters with no thought for her opinions.

"Your usual rate," she said gruffly, passing him another envelope.

"What's the job?" asked Korbuscek, relaxing a little.

The woman shrugged. "The orders are in the envelope. All I know is that you'll be going to Anza-bora Isl—"

Before she could finish the sentence, Korbuscek grabbed her by the shoulders and threw her to the floor.

A shot rang out above them, then another.

Without a word the two separated. Scuttling into the deepest shadows, Korbuscek pressed himself against a worm-eaten beam and held his breath. Three more shots were fired. But there was no cry of pain.

When enough time had passed that he was sure his contact had managed to escape, Korbuscek allowed himself a brief smile. As little as he cared for her, he would not have wanted his baby sister to be captured by these particular enemies.

Moving as silently as he had come, he left the mill, eager to read his orders.

2

The Scroungers

RAY "THE GAMMA RAY" GAMMAND RACED UP TO THE abandoned house the A.I. Gang used as a secret headquarters. Thudding to a stop, he checked his watch, then let out a sigh.

He was late again.

He tucked his beloved basketball between his knees, then took off his thick glasses and wiped them on his shirt while he caught his breath. Trying to act casual, he opened the door and stepped in.

Unfortunately, he tripped over an untied shoelace, dropped his basketball, and stumbled into the living room.

"Somebody's la-ate!" sang the handsome bronze head sitting in the middle of the coffee table.

"Shut up, Paracelsus," said Ray.

"Nobody loves me," sighed the head, which had been created by the Phillips twins, Roger and Rachel.

The twins were constantly programming Paracelsus with new remarks directed at their friends' behavior. By setting it to respond to things they expected the other kids in the gang to do, they could make its comments remarkably appropriate.

"Glad you could make it, Ray," said Trip Davis. Tall (over six feet!), slender, and intense, Trip was sitting against the wall on the opposite side of the room. To his right, in a chair that barely let her feet touch the floor, was Wendy Wendell the Third, a pint-sized dynamo the gang sometimes referred to as "the Wonderchild."

Straddling the workbench across the room from Wendy was Hap Swenson. As usual, the handsome, sturdy blond had a screwdriver in his hand and was poking away at some gadget—probably one that the Wonderchild had designed.

Sitting between Hap and Trip were the red-haired Phillips twins, who Ray thought of privately as "Volume One" and "Volume Two." This was because the twins carried so much information in their heads that between the two of them they were a virtual walking encyclopedia.

Ray sighed as he finished his inventory. That was it—all five of them. He was last again. "So what's the big emergency?" he asked.

"No emergency," said Wendy. "Just a new idea. Rachel wants us to add an optical scanner to our system. Problem is, we have to build the darn thing!" She took a bite from the enormous burger clenched between her hands and smiled blissfully. "Should be fun," she added, speaking with her mouth full.

Hap looked up from whatever he was tinkering with, scratched his blond head, and said, "You guys have got me again. Just what the heck *is* an optical scanner?"

Ray relaxed. If they hadn't explained that to Hap yet, he couldn't be *too* late. Their greaser-techie friend was the only member of the gang who didn't come from a scientific family, and they often had to fill him in on the reasoning behind their plans. The amazing thing was, he was such a whiz with tools that once they had explained something to him, he could almost always build it.

"A scanner is a device that will let us teach the computer to read," said Rachel.

"I wish someone would teach me to read!"

"Shut up, Paracelsus," said several of the kids simultaneously.

Seeing the puzzled expression that remained on Hap's face, Rachel's twin took up the explanation. "Basically, the scanner will photograph a page of printed material, then translate it into symbols the computer can understand."

"Which means we'll be able to feed information into Sherlock several times faster than we do now," put in Trip Davis.

"Sherlock" was the gang's pet project—a computer program designed to sort clues and solve crimes. Trip stood up and began pacing across the floor. His lanky frame towered over Ray, who was barely more than five feet tall. "It will be like going from a tricycle to a ten-speed as far as our programming goes," he added.

"But Sherlock won't actually *understand* what it reads," objected Hap. "Will it?"

"Of course not," said Rachel. "At least, not yet. That's what the information programming project is all about—turning that material into usable data for the computer. But right now we're wasting an enormous amount of time typing the raw stuff into the computer. The best thing would be if we had this stuff on CD-ROM or something, but, unfortunately, we don't, and with the communication blockade we can't get it without a lot of explanation. The scanner is our next best bet. It should save us a huge amount of time."

"Which means," said Wendy, tugging on one of her blond pigtails, "we might even win the race!"

The "race" Wendy was referring to had begun shortly after the head of Project Alpha, Dr. Hwa, had gathered a handful of the United States' top computer scientists at the deserted Anza-bora Island Air Force Base. Their mission: to create a "conscious" computer—a computer that could not only think, but be *aware* that it was thinking; aware, in fact, of its own existence.

Actually, the gang had started "Operation Sherlock" almost as a way of getting even for the disruption the Anza-bora project had created in their lives. With the exception of Hap, whose father had been chief mechanic for the island's recently abandoned Air Force base, the kids had all been uprooted from their homes almost without notice when their parents decided to join the project.

Even worse, it had been without explanation. Security on the project was so tight no one not actually involved in the work was supposed to know what it was about. When some clever guesswork on the gang's part tipped them off to the real reason their parents had come to Anza-bora, the kids decided to try to take a shot at the same goal.

Their initial idea had been somewhat less ambitious. It started when someone attached a small microphone to Rachel's collar during the first meeting of the top island staff and their families. The microphone had self-destructed as soon as the kids discovered it, but the incident had spurred the gang into "Operation Sherlock"—their attempt to develop a detective program that would help them sort and interpret the clues they gathered about the "bug."

It was Roger who had suggested that they go all the way and compete with their parents.

What none of them liked to talk about was the fact that since the bug had been planted at that first meeting, each one of them had at least one parent who was a prime suspect. None of them liked living with the knowledge that one (or both) of their parents might be a spy.

Even before Sherlock was operational the kids had managed to thwart a plan to blow up the island. In the process they had accidentally discovered a device designed to transmit all the work the Project Alpha scientists did to somewhere off island.

Unfortunately, like the bug on Rachel's collar, the transmitter had self-destructed before they could show it to anyone. As a result, their warnings about a spy among the project's top scientists were not being taken seriously by anyone except cranky, freckle-faced Dr. Stanley Remov.

The gang had responded to the official disbelief in the only way they could—by stepping up work on their own project. In the process, they had learned to pull together as a team.

So no one was really surprised when only four days after the meeting where the scanner was proposed, they were nearly ready to install it.

"I just need two more parts," said Hap, "and I'll have her up and running."

He tapped a few letters into the keyboard sitting next to his workbench. The keyboard was attached to the terminal (now wildly modified and upgraded) that had been left in the house when the Air Force abandoned the island.

The terminal was attached to the island's incredibly powerful mainframe, which was housed a mile or so away in the computer center.

"Good morning, Hap," said a crisp voice from across the room. "What can I do for you?"

Hap smiled. He still got a kick out of the way the others had programmed the computer's vocal simulator to sound like Basil Rathbone, the actor who had played Sherlock Holmes in so many movies.

Hap typed in a series of classified codes that Wendy

had wrangled out of the computer and called up an inventory of all the spare parts on the island. He scanned the list, then entered the codes for the items he needed.

"Those parts can be found in Warehouse Two, aisle seven, level six," said Sherlock.

"You know what that means," said Roger.

"It's scrounging time!" replied Trip with a smile.

"Major scrounge," agreed Ray.

As a team, Trip and Ray were unbeatable at turning up hard-to-locate parts. "Beg, borrow, or temporarily reposition" was their motto, though the only things they ever actually took without permission were items the Air Force had abandoned when it left the island.

Items such as those in Warehouse Two.

"Take Rinty with you," suggested Roger, gesturing to the mechanical mutt the gang had started building as a test project a few weeks earlier. "You never know. He might come in handy."

Warehouse Two was dark, and aside from the noise Ray had made tripping over a box when they first came in, so quiet it was almost eerie.

"Aisle seven should be that way," whispered Trip, shining his flashlight to their right.

Clink!

It was nothing, really; the tiniest of sounds. But when he heard it, Ray felt his stomach twist into a hard little ball. Tiny as it was, that sound had no business at all in a warehouse that was supposed to be abandoned! He switched off his flashlight and grabbed Trip's arm. "Did you hear that?" he hissed.

"I heard it," replied Trip, clicking off his own light. He licked his lips nervously, straining to see through the sudden darkness.

"What do you think it was?" asked Ray.

"I don't know. But I don't like it." Trip paused, then added, "I wish you weren't so clumsy!"

Ray felt himself blush. He hadn't meant to stumble over that box! In fact, he had been making an extra effort to be quiet.

"It's coming this way," whispered Trip. "Do me a favor and don't move!"

"I'm frozen in my tracks!"

Clink!

The sound was closer this time. Trip pressed himself against the wall, fervently wishing he had never returned *Ninja Experiments with Invisibility* to the library.

Suddenly a thin beam of light struck the floor in front of the boys.

Pretend you're a box! Ray ordered himself, flinching away from the light. *Maybe no one will notice you.*

The sound drew closer.

Why did I volunteer for this scrounging mission? wondered Trip miserably. *I could be home eating spinach.*

Trip hated spinach. But at the moment facing a plateful of the disgusting green stuff seemed infinitely preferable to being caught by whoever was prowling the warehouse.

* * *

Nervous as he was, the worst Ray was expecting was an angry member of Sergeant Brody's security force. He was wondering just how much trouble they were going to be in, when an ear-piercing blare shattered the stillness. He looked up, and began to scream. A monstrous creature with curved fangs, flashing red eyes, and a face that made sudden death seem preferable to being captured was heading straight for him, its clawlike hands stretching and grasping ahead of it.

"Run!" screamed Ray.

Trip didn't need any encouragement. He sprinted to his right like a rabbit startled by a hound.

Ray started in the opposite direction, fell over another box, scrambled to his feet, and headed between two rows of towering shelves.

Aside from the stumbling, this was all according to plan. After their first adventure, the gang had decided it would be a good idea to split in a situation like this. Then if one person got in trouble, the other could go for help.

Go for help! thought Trip. *Of course! What's the matter with my brain?*

Reaching into his pocket, he pulled out a small control device. *I sure hope this works,* he thought as he pushed the button that would send Rin Tin Stainless Steel to fetch the rest of the gang.

He was turning to look for Ray when a pair of rough hands grabbed him from behind and snatched him into the air.

3

Laughter Here, Terror There

ROGER GLANCED AT HIS WATCH. HE WAS STARTING TO worry about Trip and Ray. And he was getting peeved at Rachel, who had left forty-five minutes earlier to visit Dr. Weiskopf. This optical scanner had been her idea, and now she wouldn't even be here to help them install it.

"Rats!" exclaimed Hap, who was tinkering with something on the other side of the room. Working delicately, he pulled a broken wire from the scanner's feed unit, then rolled some fresh wire off the coil at his side. "Will somebody give me a hand with this thing?" he asked irritably as he clipped the piece of wire.

Wendy had just gotten up to help him when something began scratching at the door. Wendy moved to open it, but Norman the Doorman—a primitive butler-bot Ray had salvaged from the scrap heap—beat her to it.

"Welcome to our happy headquarters!" it said, throwing open the door.

A small metallic form dashed through, far below Norman's line of vision.

"Welcome," repeated the butler-bot.

"Arf!" yipped Rin Tin Stainless Steel. Heading straight for Wendy, the canine robot began leaping around her feet. "Arf! Arf!"

"Must have been a wrong number," said Norman, slamming the door shut.

"We gotta work on his eyesight," muttered Roger.

"Rinty, get off me!" cried Wendy, batting at the mechanical dog.

"Arf! Arf! I love you, Wendy. Will you marry me?"

"This is your work, Roger!" yelled the Wonderchild indignantly. "I'd recognize your warped sense of humor anywhere. Get this mechanical mutt off me!"

"And break his little electronic heart?" cried Roger, who was convulsed with laughter.

"Then catch!" Snatching up the yapping robot, Wendy flung it across the room.

"Cripes!" yelled Roger. Leaping to his feet, he snatched Rinty out of the air just before the little robot would have crashed into the wall.

"Watch it, Wendy!" said Hap. "You'll scramble his circuits!"

"I couldn't possibly scramble them more than Roger has already," snapped the Wonderchild.

As for Rinty, the instant Roger grabbed the robot, its gas chromatograph—an electronic nose of sorts—went into action. Sorting out the molecules that marked Roger's chemically distinctive odor, it checked their pattern against its memory banks. Within microseconds it found a match and "recognized" Roger.

Immediately a new program took over.

"Trouble!" yapped the robot. "Big trouble. Come quick!"

Rachel Phillips was sitting under a small scrub tree on the east side of Anza-bora Island. The South Pacific stretched vast and seemingly endless before her. She was not looking at the water, however, but at the shiny metal tube she held in her hands.

"Like this?" she asked, placing her fingers delicately on the holes that lined the tube.

"No, no, no!" snapped Dr. Leonard Weiskopf, the little man sitting next to her. "Hold it like you mean business. You're not going to break it!"

Rachel brushed a strand of her fiery red hair away from her damp forehead.

"Come, come, Rachel," said Dr. Weiskopf. "Pay attention to the business at hand!"

The business at hand was learning to use a pennywhistle, the cheap tin instrument Dr. Weiskopf was able to play with amazing skill and beauty. When Rachel had first approached the balding scientist about teaching her, he had been delighted at the prospect. Unfortunately, he was not always as patient as Rachel would have liked.

"Let me show you again," he said, raising his own whistle to his lips. His hands, strangely large for such a small man, almost hid the tiny instrument.

Rachel wondered how he could make those sausagelike fingers move so swiftly over the whistle's holes; they became a near blur whenever he hurtled through some fast-paced piece of classical musical. Now, however, he piped a slower tune, closing his eyes and swaying gently with the music. A stray breeze wafting in from the ocean stirred the fringe of gray hair that circled his shiny head.

He seemed so lost in what he was playing that Rachel wondered if he had forgotten she was there. *How peaceful he looks,* she thought, remembering the impatient tones that had marked his voice just moments earlier. "What is it about music that can calm someone so?"

"I beg your pardon?" said Dr. Weiskopf, lowering the pennywhistle.

Rachel blushed; she hadn't intended to speak aloud.

"I . . . I was just noticing how content you seemed while you were playing that tune. I wondered what it was about music that calmed people like that."

" 'Music hath charms to soothe the savage beast'?" asked Dr. Weiskopf.

"Breast," corrected Rachel.

"I beg your pardon?"

"The correct quote is 'Music has charms to soothe a savage *breast.*' It's from William Congreve's 'The Mourning Bride'—Act 1, Scene 1. People usually misquote it."

Dr. Weiskopf looked at her strangely.

"I have sort of an overactive memory," she explained, blushing a little. "Anyway, the point is, if you're any kind of an example, the quote is true. A minute ago you were . . ."

She began to blush again.

Dr. Weiskopf laughed. "Oh, come right out and say it. I was cranky. Then I played some music and calmed right down. It's true, music can do that. But it can also rile things up. And if you don't recognize that, you're only dealing with half the truth. Give me the right song, and I can start a war."

Rachel raised a questioning eyebrow.

"Soldiers always have their battle songs. I have a historian friend who claims that if the South had had an anthem as inspiring as 'The Battle Hymn of the Republic,' they might have won the Civil War. That's the other face of music—its dark side, if you will. Everything has one, you know."

"You can't shine a light without casting some shadows," said Rachel, quoting her father's favorite response to people who complained about problems created by modern science.

"Precisely!" exclaimed Weiskopf. "You're a very sensible young lady, Miss Phillips." He leaned toward Rachel. "Can you keep a secret?"

Rachel had the uncomfortable feeling he was trying to look inside her head, to see if he could trust her. She licked her lips nervously. What was going on here?

"I said, can you keep a secret? Oh, come along—I know you can! You and your friends have got all kinds of secrets going on. You're the most closemouthed group of kids I ever saw!"

"How did you know that?" asked Rachel indignantly.

Dr. Weiskopf seemed flustered for a moment. "Dr. Remov told me," he said at last.

Dr. Remov was another of the Project Alpha scientists, one the gang had turned to for help during their first adventure. Rachel didn't like the fact that he had mentioned their conversations to anyone else.

"I can keep a secret," she said after a moment. Then she added: "Better than some adults, it would seem."

It was Dr. Weiskopf's turn to blush. "Stanley had his reasons for talking to me. Believe me, I have not mentioned what he told me to anyone else. Perhaps you could consider what I want to show you a trade—secret for secret."

"What is it?" asked Rachel. An eager note had crept into her voice, for despite her cautious nature, Dr. Weiskopf had made her curious.

"Patience," said the scientist, holding up a finger. "All will be revealed in a few moments."

Rachel thought she was going to burst by the time they entered Dr. Weiskopf's bungalow—one of the multitude of Air Force buildings that had been left behind when the government abandoned Anza-bora Island.

"All right," said Dr. Weiskopf once they were standing in his living room, "stand here and watch." Raising his whistle to his lips, he played a little tune. Though it couldn't have been more than twelve notes long, Rachel found it oddly moving.

"What . . ."

Dr. Weiskopf held up a hand to silence her.

Rachel heard a sound from the other room.

The door swung open.

To Dr. Weiskopf's dismay, Rachel broke into gales of laughter.

Trip Davis squirmed desperately as he tried to escape the hands that had grabbed him. *I wonder if Ray got away,* he thought as he slammed his right foot backward. He connected with something firm but fleshy, and the satisfying grunt of pain that followed made it clear his captor was at least human.

Trying to remember the self-defense lessons Wendy had given him, Trip reached over his shoulder. A few minutes of confusion, angry shouts, and loud thumping noises followed.

Then it was all over.

On the other side of the warehouse the Gamma Ray had taken cover behind a pair of huge wooden crates, where he was having second thoughts about the gang's "split up in an emergency" policy. The idea that someone should escape to go for help was good in theory. On the other hand, considering the look of the thing that had sent him running, there might not be much of him left to help when the others did get here.

Ray's second thoughts turned to dead certainty when he peeked around the edge of a crate and saw that the red-eyed monstrosity had chosen to come after him instead of Trip. No question about it: He did not want to face that thing alone!

Spurred by fear, he shot from between the crates

and hurtled down a narrow canyon formed by stacks of boxes. *What is that thing, anyway?* he wondered as he raced around a corner. *Where did it come from?*

He ducked through a small passage on his right, hoping to lose the relentless pursuer. His breath was getting short and a throbbing pain was tying knots in his side. He couldn't go on much longer!

Glancing fearfully over his shoulder, Ray was relieved to see that he had broken away. But looking back was a mistake, for with his next step he stumbled over a box and sprawled facedown on the floor. His glasses went flying out in front of him.

As he scrambled for them, he heard a whirring noise behind him.

Behind that, he heard a deep laugh.

Who's back there? he wondered.

A chill shivered along his spine. *What if Black Glove has come back?*

He searched desperately for his glasses, his hands scuttling over the floor like a pair of spastic spiders.

Where are they? Crawling forward, he bumped against another box. It rattled.

He could hear his pursuer closing in behind him.

The box was open. He thrust his hands into it, on the chance that his glasses might have fallen inside.

Ball bearings!

Without an instant's hesitation, he turned the box over and sent several thousand perfect metal spheres rolling across the floor.

A shout of anger let him know his move had scored.

But before he could congratulate himself, he was plucked from the floor by a pair of metallic hands.

Even without his glasses, Ray knew he was face-to-face with the red-eyed monstrosity that had been pursuing him.

Ignoring the treacherous curves in the road, Roger pushed his dune buggy to the limits of its speed. They had to get to Trip and Ray!

His sense of urgency was fueled by the guilt he felt over tampering with Rinty's program. He was painfully aware that his lighthearted joke had delayed the delivery of the computerized canine's vital message. Not by more than thirty seconds, of course. But the last mess the gang had been in had taught Roger all too well that half a minute could mean the difference between life and death.

The dune buggy bounced on. Because its electric motor was completely silent, the only sound was the complaining of the springs and an occasional screech as they rounded a sharp curve.

I should have left well enough alone, he thought. *It's just that Wendy's so much fun to tease!*

Of course, that was partly because it was so easy. The slightest thing could set her off; Hap had once called the Wonderchild a "four-foot stick of dynamite with a two-inch fuse." And the little twerp was really cute when she got angry.

"Watch where you're going!" cried Hap.

Roger focused on the road and spun the steering

wheel sharply to the right. The dune buggy swerved, bounced in a rut, and barely missed slamming into a roadside tree.

"Close one, good buddy!" said Hap, as calmly as if he were describing a near miss in a game of marbles. "Better keep your mind on the road."

"Sorry about that," said Roger sheepishly. He was glad Wendy wasn't in the buggy with them. Then he would never hear the end of it.

As it was, she was bouncing along in her own duner right behind them. So she had undoubtedly seen his near miss. She'd probably still suggest he needed a CAT scan to see if there was a bolt or two loose in his brain.

"Turn here," said Hap, pointing to the left. "There's a back way to the warehouse over there."

The dune buggy bounced across the uneven ground, and soon they pulled up outside Warehouse Two.

Wendy skidded to a stop beside them.

Three Jeeps, marked with the insignia of the island's security patrol, were already parked outside the building. Sitting in one of them, looking as angry as they had ever seen him, was Dr. Hwa.

"Wait! Where do you think you're going?" he yelled as the three youngsters sprinted past him for the warehouse door. They ignored him. The scientist might be the island's head honcho, but when their friends needed help, that didn't mean a thing.

Roger threw open the door, and the three kids burst into the warehouse.

4

Robots

"I'M SORRY, DR. WEISKOPF!" SPUTTERED RACHEL AS
she tried to catch her breath. "I just wasn't expecting
anything like . . . like . . . th-th-this!"

She exploded in laughter again.

The "this" she was referring to was a barrel-shaped
robot with a five-by-five grid of flashing, multicolored
lights centered on its chest. From its base jutted three
stubby cylinders with wheels on their bottoms.

All of this was standard, if a little clumsy in its styl-
ing. What had set Rachel to laughing was the robot's
face, which was unmistakably modeled after the great
composer Ludwig van Beethoven. The bizarre contrast between the robot's face and its body was what
had started her laughing fit. The startled look on Dr.
Weiskopf's face had kept it going. Now no matter how
she tried, she couldn't stop.

Looking mournful, Dr. Weiskopf raised his pennywhistle and played a little tune. The robot pivoted and began to roll out of the room.

"Wait!" cried Rachel. The robot didn't stop.

She took a deep breath. Using all her willpower, she forced herself to hold it. Her lungs were almost ready to explode when she felt another burst of laughter coming on. She clamped her mouth shut, feeling as if she were trying to hold in a massive, inevitable sneeze. For an instant she was afraid the top of her head might blow off.

Slowly she released the air from her lungs, then took another deep breath. She did this three times, then said softly, "Sorry. I'm all right now."

Dr. Weiskopf looked at her carefully. Still not speaking, he placed the whistle to his lips and resummoned the robot.

When it rolled back into the room Dr. Weiskopf said, "Rachel, I'd like you to meet Euterpe."

Rachel bit the inside corners of her mouth and tried desperately not to break into a new fit of giggling. What a name to drop on someone trying to keep a straight face!

Stop it! she commanded herself. *I absolutely forbid you to start laughing again!*

After a brief struggle, she was in control, despite the absurd name. Then she remembered that she had heard it before and decided perhaps it wasn't quite so ridiculous after all.

"Euterpe—wasn't she the muse of music in Greek mythology?"

"Very good," said Dr. Weiskopf. "As you will see, the name was chosen for a reason. Let me show you what she can do."

Positioning himself in front of Euterpe, he took out his pennywhistle again. The grid of lights on the robot's chest was glowing, but so faintly as to be barely discernible. Dr. Weiskopf put the whistle to his lips and piped a single, pure note.

How does he do that? wondered Rachel. She had tried for days now, and still could not get the wobble out of her tones.

Before she had time to give the matter much thought, the robot answered its creator, repeating the tone perfectly. The sound was pretty, but nothing very impressive. That kind of programming had been available for years.

Dr. Weiskopf played another note.

Euterpe answered.

The scientist played a series of five tones.

The robot repeated them perfectly.

Rachel was beginning to wonder what this was all about when Dr. Weiskopf started to play a tune. To her astonishment, the robot began to sing along with him—not merely repeating the notes, but working in harmony!

Dr. Weiskopf glanced sideways. Catching Rachel's eye, he raised his own eyebrow, as if to ask, *"Now* are you impressed?" Then he returned his attention to the music. He began to play faster, as if testing the limits of the robot's ability. Euterpe kept pace with him. Soon the grid of lights on the robot's chest began to flash, creating a rhythm and pattern that seemed to match the music.

Then, suddenly, Euterpe's notes went soaring above Dr. Weiskopf's in a thrilling descant. The sound was like nothing Rachel had ever heard before, some strange combination of a human voice and a flute. No—wait. Now it was like a trumpet, quavering, hovering over a note, then diving onto it and carrying it down with a series of trills into a deep bass tone that sent a shiver trembling down her spine.

Dr. Weiskopf was sweating now, as if it was all he could do to keep up with his robot. Euterpe's lights flashed merrily, including a pair that shone forth from the eyes in the Beethoven-like face.

The duet (or duel—Rachel was never quite sure which it was) went on until Dr. Weiskopf finally put down his whistle and wiped his brow. Euterpe went right on playing, toying with the themes its creator had offered, trying variations, using different tones and voices.

The music was so beautiful that Rachel hugged herself with pleasure.

"I'm glad you like it," said Dr. Weiskopf softly. "Of course, that's not what I've really designed her for. It's just a little trick that works off her main program."

"*Little* trick?" asked Rachel.

"Oh, yes." Dr. Weiskopf smiled. "Her real purpose is much greater. You might even say it's . . . cosmic!"

Roger could hardly believe his eyes. The sight of Trip Davis standing over a burly security guard who was cradling his head in his hands and moaning softly was strange enough. But the fierce-looking robot rolling in slow circles while a bellowing Ray Gammand tried to escape from its metallic clutches was almost beyond belief.

It would also have been amusing, if Ray was not so clearly terrified. What *was* amusing was the sight of Staff Sergeant Artemus P. Brody—head of the island's security force and no fan of the A.I. Gang—trying to get his footing on a floor full of ball bearings.

Roger winced as Brody's feet went flying out from under him and he crashed to the floor with the full force of his two hundred pounds.

Brody's bellow of anger was cut off by a sharp voice from behind them. "Sergeant Brody, stop this nonsense and get to your feet at once!"

It was Dr. Hwa.

Brody scrambled to his feet and snapped his boss a salute. Immediately his legs flew out from under him, and he hit the deck again. Fortunately for Brody, he landed on the most well-padded portion of his body.

"Sergeant Brody!" snapped Hwa again.

The furious tone in his voice bothered Roger; it didn't sound right coming from the usually calm scientist.

Like the rest of the kids, Roger was fond of the diminutive Dr. Hwa. Even if he wouldn't take their warnings as seriously as they would have wished, he had done everything he could to make their stay on Anza-bora Island pleasant, including providing them with access to everything from dune buggies to the main computer itself. What's more, he was almost always willing to talk to them, despite the protective nature of his fierce secretary, Bridget McGrory. To top it off, Dr. Hwa had a great deal of personal charm; he was the kind of man other people just naturally wanted to be with.

Now, however, his voice sounded not only angry but bone-weary. It was clear that the strain of managing Project Alpha was getting to him. Considering the recent security violations he had had to deal with, that was hardly a surprise. Roger hoped it wouldn't end up breaking the man.

"Sorry, Dr. Hwa," panted Brody, crawling from the midst of the ball bearings on his hands and knees. His face was beet red, though whether from anger or exertion was hard to tell.

"Get me outta here!" bellowed the Gamma Ray. "NOW!"

The robot clutching him continued to roll in circles.

Brody lumbered to his feet and pulled a black object the size of a deck of cards from his pocket. He punched a button.

The robot started to move faster.

"Stop this thing!" screamed Ray.

Brody stared at the remote control and scratched his head. Finally he pushed another button. The robot stopped rolling. At the touch of a third button, it spread its mechanical arms and dumped the Gamma Ray unceremoniously to the floor.

Brody chuckled maliciously.

Hap went over and helped the smaller boy to his feet.

"Would somebody care to tell me just what is going on here?" asked Dr. Hwa, his voice crisp with anger.

Six voices began speaking at the same time.

"Stop!" cried Dr. Hwa, clutching his head. "One at a time!" Looking around, he made a quick decision. "Roger, you seem to be the spokesperson for your group. We'll start with you."

Roger licked his lips nervously and began rubbing his thumb and forefinger together, a sure sign that his brain was moving into high gear. "Well, it was like this, Dr. Hwa," he said slowly. "We were working on a little gadget—"

"What kind of gadget?" asked Brody.

Roger shrugged. "Just something to help us with our programming. Actually, my sister dreamed it up."

When Brody nodded in satisfaction Roger had to hide his smile. He had added the bit about Rachel because he knew Brody was so blindly convinced of male superiority he would automatically dismiss anything thought up by a female.

"Anyway, we had almost finished making it when we realized we were missing an important part—"

"What kind of part?"

Roger cast a long-suffering look at Dr. Hwa.

"Sergeant Brody, let the young man tell the story in his own way," said the scientist. He sounded like a weary judge reprimanding an overzealous lawyer.

Brody scowled, but held his tongue. Dr. Hwa nodded to Roger to continue.

"Since we needed this part before we could do anything else, Trip and Ray volunteered to go out on a scrounge. We knew there were all kinds of spare parts left in this warehouse when the Air Force pulled out, so it seemed a logical place to start."

"This is government property!" sputtered Brody.

"It's been abandoned," said Roger coolly. He put out a hand to steady the Wonderchild, who seemed on the verge of exploding with exasperation. "As I was *trying* to explain," he continued, casting a significant look at Brody, "the guys came here to look for the part. Next thing we knew, we had a message asking for help, so we came on the double. When we got here, we found our friends had been attacked by one of Brody's men and this robot goon. That's all I know. But I sure would be interested in finding out why that robot is here." He paused, then added, "I bet our parents would, too."

Dr. Hwa looked unhappy at this comment. The last thing he wanted was to antagonize any of his key researchers. "The robots were Sergeant Brody's idea," he said. A note of resignation colored his voice, as if he really didn't care for the things himself. "He ordered them after last month's security problems."

"Newest thing in protective services," said Brody proudly. "Loaded with all kinds of sensors. 'Deathmonger' here can detect body heat from a hundred feet away. They have infrared devices to let them see in the dark, ultrasensitive sound detectors—"

"Don't they end up chasing rats?" asked Roger innocently.

"Brody had better watch out if they do," muttered Wendy. "He'll be the first one they carry off."

Sergeant Brody glared at the Wonderchild. He hadn't quite made out her words, but he was sure that whatever she had said was an insult. He turned back to Roger. "No, they don't chase rats. At least, not most of the time. The programming is pretty good at deciding which sounds are important."

"Why are they so fierce looking?" asked Ray angrily.

"It's psychological," said Brody, puffing out his chest.

"Jeez," whispered Wendy. "He learned a new word."

Roger elbowed her to be silent. "You mean it makes you feel better to have something that looks like that on your side?" he asked sweetly.

Brody scowled at him. "No, it makes an intruder feel worse! You see something like Deathmonger rolling at you out of the darkness, and it's apt to freeze you in your tracks for a minute."

"I can vouch for that," said Trip. "I think the thing scared me out of a year's growth."

Since Trip had already passed the six-foot mark, this complaint didn't generate much sympathy—especially not from Wendy and Ray.

"I don't care much for it myself," said Dr. Hwa. "I don't like to see the noble science of robotics used in such a fashion. Unfortunately, after what happened last month, Sergeant Brody's request seemed a necessary evil."

Roger felt sorry for Dr. Hwa. Clearly the man would prefer to concentrate on Project Alpha and ignore the problems with security. But as head of the project, he had no choice but to deal with these things.

Too bad he got saddled with a beefhead like Brody to run security, thought Roger. According to what his father had told him, Brody had been part of the deal when the government agreed to turn Anza-bora Island over to Project Alpha. That wasn't surprising; even though this was a private operation, the government was vitally interested in its outcome, and wanted the research kept secure. To get the island, poor Dr. Hwa had been forced to accept Brody along with it.

"Sergeant Brody has also requisitioned additional human guards for the island," said Dr. Hwa dismally.

"Got eight more men coming in today," said Brody proudly. Glaring at the kids, he added, "That ought to take care of things around here."

Even as Sergeant Brody was bragging to the A.I. Gang about his new security men, the weekly delivery plane was touching down on the Anza-bora airstrip.

The plane carried the island's usual supplies: food, various computer components, and a mass of scientific journals and papers detailing the latest findings in any area that might be of the slightest interest to the Project Alpha scientists. They came this way, instead of over the electronic web through which most computer scientists stayed in contact, because of the communications blackout.

34

After all, no hacker, no matter how brilliant, could break into a computer that had no phone lines connected to it.

The plane taxied to a halt in front of Warehouse Four, where a pair of robo-trucks began the unloading process.

Normally this entire operation would be accomplished mechanically; security was so tight the pilot and copilot were not even allowed to disembark.

This time, however, the plane carried something more than the usual cargo. Even as the crates were being unloaded from the back, the passenger door opened and a ramp extended to the ground.

Marching in single file, Sergeant Brody's eight carefully selected security guards disembarked from the plane.

Seventh in line was the spy named Ramon Korbuscek.

Korbuscek seemed to fit perfectly with the seven other men as they marched to their new quarters. But then, he would never stand out in a crowd; it was one of his gifts to be able to blend in almost anywhere. The only difference between him and the others was the constant movement of his eyes back and forth as he memorized small details of his new territory.

While it would have been hard to quantify exactly, Korbuscek knew he was probably seeing at least twice as much as any other man in the line. Not things they couldn't see; just things they didn't bother to see. He had learned long ago that his life depended on such details. Combined with a fierce and powerful mind and a ruthless devotion to a cause—whatever cause happened to be paying him at the moment—his talent for observing, retaining, and interpreting details was part of what made him one of the highest paid agents in international intelligence.

The group turned right and entered a medium-sized building, where the guard on duty assigned them to their quarters. Korbuscek was pleased: only two men to a room. That meant he would have a lot of privacy.

He would have even more once he got his roommate transferred to another room—or thrown off the island altogether.

He threw his duffel bag at the foot of the bed and stretched out on the mattress.

"I'm going for a cup of coffee," said his new roommate. "Want to come along?"

Korbuscek shook his head. "I'm going to sack out for a while," he said, feigning a yawn. "With my luck, I'll have night patrol—starting tonight!"

The other man shrugged. "Suit yourself. But don't forget we've got a meeting with the island bigwigs in two hours."

"Almost slipped my mind," lied Korbuscek, who in reality never forgot anything. "Wake me if I'm asleep, would you?"

The other man grinned. "Sure. No sense in getting off to a bad start." He closed the door behind him as he left the room. His roommate seemed a tad strange. Even so he had a feeling he was going to like him.

This was not surprising. Ramon Korbuscek could make almost anyone like him, if it suited his purposes.

Lying on his bunk, Korbuscek mentally reviewed the layout of the island as he had seen it so far. Then he closed his eyes and repeated to himself the instructions about his mission—instructions having to do with a certain Dr. Leonard Weiskopf, and a robot named Euterpe.

5

The Music of the Spheres

"WE'VE GOTTA DO SOMETHING ABOUT BRODY'S RO-bots," said Roger, pacing back and forth across the living room of the gang's headquarters. "Those things could really slow down our work!"

"You're not kidding," said Hap fervently. "I almost fell over when Brody told you he had ordered another twenty-five of those monstrosities. The man is sick!"

"He reads too much cheap science fiction!" yelled Wendy from the kitchen, where she was cooking a burger. "It's warped his mind!"

Wendy was the reason the gang even had a functioning kitchen. Once they realized how cranky she got if she had to endure the entire time from one meal to another without gorging on something in between, they had restored the stove and sink to working order for their own protection.

Ray, who was sitting on his basketball, was about to make a point when Rachel burst through the door. "Have I got news for you guys!" she shouted.

"Will it keep?" asked Roger. "We've got trouble."

Rachel knew her twin well enough to tell that he was serious. She glanced around at the group of worried faces and noticed one missing. "Wendy!" she cried. "Something's happened to Wendy!"

As the more cautious of the gang's two females, Rachel was constantly worried that the Wonderchild's impetuosity would land her in serious trouble.

"Nah, I'm fine," said Wendy, emerging from the kitchen with a huge multilayered something in her hand.

"What is *that?"* asked Trip.

"Megaburger," she replied, taking an enormous bite. " 'Sgood!"

The Gamma Ray shook his head. He was dying to ask what was in it, but Wendy's appetite—remarkable even at its best—had taken a turn for the bizarre lately. If he had to watch her eat, he decided he'd just as soon not know what it was.

Rachel rolled her eyes. "I should have known better than to worry about you. So what *is* the big problem?"

Roger gave his twin a quick rundown of what had happened in the warehouse. His story was punctuated by frequent interruptions from Trip and Ray, especially when he described Brody's new robot.

"I felt like I was trapped in one of my father's games," said Ray mournfully.

When they were done, Rachel said, "Obviously we have to design a remote-control device that will override their command system."

"We'd have to be able to examine one of them to do that," objected Hap. "Study its circuits and so on."

"So we borrow one for a while," said Rachel with a shrug.

"I don't think you understand," said Trip. "The whole problem with these things is that they're going to *keep* us from borrowing stuff."

"Not to mention that they're about as friendly as a werewolf at full moon," said Ray.

Rachel was unconvinced. "Look, those things came on you when you were totally unprepared. Now we know they're here, and we have a good sense of what their capabilities are. If we're as bright as we think we are, we ought to be able to use that information to bait a little trap for one of Brody's new toys."

"She's right!" said Ray after a second. "Half the reason I got so scared is that I wasn't expecting the thing. We've been acting like it's going to be a surprise every time we see one. But it's not. I think we can do it."

"All right," said Roger. "I'm sold. Our next job is to capture a robot!"

"No," said Rachel. "Our next job is to visit one. I've got something I want to show you."

*   *   *

With the gang gathered in a knot behind her, Rachel pressed the doorbell of Dr. Weiskopf's house.

No answer.

She pressed again.

No answer.

Finally she looked back at the others and shrugged. "It's all right. Dr. Weiskopf said we should feel free to go on in if he's not here. Come on, we'll get the emergency key."

Leading the others to the back of the house, Rachel knelt beside the back steps and picked up a stone that turned out to be made of plastic.

"Cute, but probably not very effective," said Wendy as Rachel removed the key from the fake rock. "Doesn't this guy know there's a real spy on the island?"

"Probably not," said Ray. "Outside of Dr. Remov, no one seems to believe us. Why should Dr. Weiskopf be any different? The adults all want to believe the place is one big happy family."

"Then why bother to lock the door at all?" asked Hap as Rachel opened the door and led them into the house.

"Basic psychology," replied Trip, pushing back a lock of his blond hair. "People always worry, even if they don't think there's anything to worry about. It's called floating anxieties. Locking the door makes a person feel more secure."

"Okay, now just stand here," said Rachel when they were all gathered in the living room. Smiling mysteriously, she took her pennywhistle from her pocket and played the twelve-note tune Dr. Weiskopf had taught her.

Euterpe came rolling into the room.

Rachel tried to scowl down the burst of snorts and giggles that greeted the robot's arrival.

"What's its name?" asked Hap, trying to keep a straight face.

"Euterpe."

Wendy whooped with delight. "Me Tarzan, you Twerpy!" she yelled.

"Terpy," said Rachel severely. "The name is Euterpe—*without* the *w!*"

But the damage was done. Once Wendy had suggested the name, none of them was able to think of the robot as anything but "Twerpy."

"Okay, so what makes this bucket of bolts so special?" asked the Gamma Ray. He was standing next to the robot, examining the light board in its chest. "Tight construction," he muttered to himself, checking the welding work.

"Listen," said Rachel. "I'll demonstrate."

She put the pennywhistle to her lips and played another tune.

Nothing happened.

"Rats. I must have done it wrong. Let me try again."

She paused for a moment, trying to remember the exact combination of notes that would call up the program she was after. Closing her eyes, she tried to hear them as Dr. Weiskopf had played them.

She tried again.

Nothing.

Her frown deepened. This was getting embarrassing—especially after the way she had babbled on about Euterpe while she was dragging the others over here.

"How sensitive is its hearing?" asked Wendy.

"Very, I think," said Rachel. "Why?"

"Your flute is flat."

Rachel blushed. She would have been more jealous of Wendy's gift of perfect pitch if she had not been well aware that the Wonderchild was equally envious of her own highly trained memory.

"I'll try again," she said. Tightening her lips, she concentrated on creating the purest tones possible.

A moment after she put down the whistle, Euterpe's eyes flashed on.

The lights on its chest began to flicker on and off.

And then the robot began to sing.

The youngsters listened, spellbound. Euterpe's song was unlike anything they had ever heard before. It had an eerie quality that gave them goose bumps. Yet there was something strangely familiar about it; something as ancient as time, something else as new as tomorrow.

The robot's voice was nearly human, though its range was far greater than any human voice, with clear, flutelike tones at the top and rumbling bass notes so deep they were felt rather than heard. Its eyes flashed on and off as it sang, and the grid of lights on its chest worked in ever-changing patterns. The song went on, never repeating itself, always new, though the same motifs sounded over and over in varying combinations.

Trip felt the small hairs rising on the back of his neck. "What is she playing? he asked.

"The music of the spheres," said Rachel happily. Lifting her flute, she played a five-note signal that commanded Euterpe to end its concert.

The music did not end abruptly. Rather the robot played on for a moment, drawing the threads of the piece together, combining them in a climax that thundered out, then dwindled softly to the high, pure sound of a flute.

For a moment all was silent. Then the gang broke into spontaneous applause, in tribute to both the robot and its creator.

"Okay," said Hap after a moment. "So what is the 'music of the spheres'?"

"It's an old idea," said Roger. "A mystical thing about the perfect sound made by the movement of the heavenly bodies."

"And that's just what this is," said Rachel. "Except it's not mystical."

"Plasmodic," said Wendy. "Only I'm still confused."

"It took me a while to get it, too," said Rachel. "Dr. Weiskopf has programmed in the motions of everything in the solar system—the planets, their moons, even the asteroids and the comets. Then Euterpe uses this incredibly complex program he created to translate that information into music. The harmonies are based on the relationship of the 'spheres' to each other *at the very moment that she's playing.* That's why the music is always different: The raw material is constantly changing."

"So what she just played for us really *was* the music of the spheres!" cried Roger in delight. "That is utterly cool!"

"But what good is it?" asked Hap.

"Art doesn't have to do anything practical," said Trip, sounding disgusted.

"Oh, but this does do something practical," said Rachel. "What's the biggest problem in space right now?"

"Junk," replied Wendy instantly.

"Right! Now, if you—"

"Wait a minute!" said Hap. "I'm just a grease monkey, remember? I make cars run and stuff like that. So fill me in. What the heck are you talking about?"

"Cut the false modesty," said Rachel. "You're 'just a grease monkey' the way Leonardo da Vinci was just a paint splasher."

"All right, so I exaggerated," said Hap, trying not to let Rachel's' compliment paste a dippy grin across his face. "I still don't know what you're talking about."

"Space junk," said Ray. "In the last few decades we've launched so many satellites that heaven is getting crowded."

"That doesn't make any sense. The one thing I do know about space is how much there is of it. How can it get crowded?"

"Well, we're not talking about space in the grand

sense," said Rachel. "Just the small patch of it around our planet."

"That's still billions of cubic miles!" protested Hap.

"True," said Ray. "But the situation is complicated by the fact that the best routes for communications satellites are limited—and nearly filled."

"And there are no controls on those routes," added Trip. "Because no one can agree who should be in charge, or what the rules should be. So private companies all over the world are putting up satellites anywhere they want to. Plug in the fact that once a satellite is no longer useful, it tends to stay in orbit for a long time, and you get a real mess for those who are trying to put new satellites into useful positions."

"Okay, you've convinced me," said Hap. "But what does that have to do with Twerpy?"

Rachel put her hand on the robot's head and smiled. "Right now it makes music based on the motions of the planets—primarily because that's the information that Dr. Weiskopf fed into it. But launched into space, where its detectors can pick up the motion of all the satellites whirling around up there, it could do the same thing: create harmonic patterns based on their motions."

"What good does that do?" asked Wendy.

"I think I know!" cried Trip. "The program works both ways. Not only can Euterpe create harmonies based on their movement, it can make their movements harmonious!"

"Translated, that means the program could keep

them from running into each other, or interfering with each other," said Roger.

"Exactly," said Rachel.

"Brilliant!" cried Ray.

Rachel smiled. *Too bad Dr. Weiskopf isn't here to see their reaction,* she thought.

To her surprise, a familiar voice behind her said, "Thank you. Euterpe and I are both very gratified—especially since no one else seems to appreciate us."

"Dr. Weiskopf!" cried Rachel, spinning around. Her delight in seeing him gave way to a puzzled frown. "What do you mean, no one seems to appreciate you?"

Dr. Weiskopf shook his head. A bitter expression crossed his face. "I just came back from a meeting with Dr. Hwa. He vetoed my request to take Euterpe to the U.S. Space Committee."

"Why?" cried Rachel.

The scientist slumped into a chair and shook his head wearily. "Good reasons, I suppose. At least, good from Dr. Hwa's point of view." He raised his hand and began to tick off the points on his oversize fingers. "First, he doesn't want the publicity. As far as Dr. Hwa is concerned, the less attention we get, the better. Second, and more important, he's afraid it would interfere with my work on ADAM. Third, he thinks—"

"Back up a second," said Roger. "What's ADAM?"

Dr. Weiskopf's eyes widened, and a hint of a blush colored his cheeks. "It's a classified term," he said at last. He paused, seemed to debate with himself for a moment, then said, "Oh, I don't see what it can hurt. It's not as if you can tell anyone about it! ADAM is the name we've given to the main computer. It stands for Advanced Design for Artificial Mentality."

"Good name for an artificial intelligence project," said Rachel. She started to add that she liked the idea of naming the new form of intelligent life the Project Alpha team was trying to create after the biblical first man. Just in time she remembered that the gang wasn't supposed to know the project was trying to create a computer that was actually *conscious* of its intelligence, and bit back her words.

Dr. Weiskopf looked at her oddly, then said, "Anyway, Dr. Hwa doesn't want me distracted from my work on ADAM. I tried to explain that they were related but it didn't seem to impress him. The bottom line is, Euterpe is grounded."

"That's not fair!" cried Wendy. "You've done something spectacular. It deserves to be used."

Dr. Weiskopf spread his enormous hands in a gesture of despair. "I agree. But Dr. Hwa is in charge, and he pretty much gave me my choice: Take this to the Space Committee or work on Project Alpha. I can't do both. And my primary commitment *is* to the computer team."

He let his hands slip into his lap.

"Well, there's only one thing to do," said Rachel. She waited, smiling mysteriously.

"All right, I'll bite," said Hap after a moment of silence. "What is it?"

6

The Warning

RACHEL'S SMILE GREW BROADER. "WE BUILD A ROCKET and launch Euterpe ourselves!"

Wendy snorted. "Come on, Rachel. Get real."

"I am being real!"

"Of course she is!" exclaimed Trip, turning to the others. "It's not like we would have to design the rocket all by ourselves or work out the mathematics for the launch ratios and the orbit patterns, or whatever. The computer is chock full of sophisticated design functions."

"And we wouldn't be doing it completely on our own," pointed out Rachel. "After all, we've got one of the most brilliant scientists in the world to work with." She turned to Dr. Weiskopf. "Haven't we?"

The little scientist was looking at her with genuine alarm.

"Don't you think we can do it?" asked Rachel.

Dr. Weiskopf spread his hands. "But Dr. Hwa . . ." he said helplessly.

"Oh, let Dr. Hwa build his own rocket," said Wendy, now won over by Rachel's idea. "He had his chance and he blew it."

"What can Dr. Hwa say?" asked Roger, taking a more diplomatic approach. "As long as you don't let this interfere with your work on Project Alpha, he has no grounds for complaint. Besides, this way he won't have to worry about the Space Committee trying to lure you away."

"Even if that were true, how would you build such a thing?" asked Dr. Weiskopf. "It's one thing to design it, quite another to make it real."

"But that's what's so great about this idea!" cried Trip, who loved new projects. "I bet there's not a better place in the world to try something like this. Where are we? On an abandoned Air Force base. And what did the Air Force do here? Oh, lots of things—but mostly test new types of aircraft, including missiles and rocket planes. This whole island is set up for that kind of work." He paused, then added with a devilish grin, "And I know where there's a whole warehouse full of spare parts!"

"I bet I can get my dad to help us," said Hap, catching Trip's enthusiasm. "He loves to build things. We'll have to design it, of course. But he'll help with the hands-on stuff, which would be mostly my job anyway. It won't make any difference to him whether Dr. Hwa wants us to build it. He's still employed by the government. As long as he does his job at the motor pool, what he does on his own time is his business."

"This is great!" exclaimed Ray. "We'll have Twerpy in orbit before Dr. Hwa knows what hit him!"

"Twerpy?" asked Dr. Weiskopf. He sounded deeply offended.

Rachel blushed. "She seems to have picked up a nickname."

"Yeah," put in Wendy, who had never been known to blush for any reason. "When you stick a name like 'Euterpe' on something, you have to expect people to mess around with it a little."

"But that name is perfect for what she does!" exclaimed Dr. Weiskopf. "Euterpe was the muse of music. It's a name filled with history, with dignity; a name honored among composers everywhere. I even keyed her command system to my pennywhistle because the muse Euterpe was usually depicted carrying a flute."

Typical scientist, thought Hap. *Suggest we build a rocket to send his creation into space and he gets a little nervous. Start fiddling with the* name *of that creation and he goes bananas!*

"Anyway," continued Dr. Weiskopf, "while I appreciate your enthusiasm, the whole idea is pointless. Without the cooperation of the Space Committee, Euterpe would have no control functions, so she couldn't affect the orbits of the other satellites anyway."

"Could she still plot them out?" asked Rachel.

"Well, yes . . ."

"Then you'd have a demonstration of what she could do! That's what counts at this stage."

Dr. Weiskopf looked a little confused. "I suppose that's true," he said reluctantly.

"Just think of it, sir," said Roger, putting one arm around Dr. Weiskopf's shoulder and sweeping the other skyward. "Imagine Euterpe sailing through the heavens, creating beautiful harmonies to send back to earth. It wouldn't be just the control of the satellites. It would be the music—new music that no one has ever heard before. That's what she was made for!"

"It's true," said Dr. Weiskopf, a dreamy look on his face. "That is what she was made for."

"Then it's settled!" crowed Rachel. "You'll never regret this, Dr. Weiskopf."

"I think I'm regretting it already," said Dr. Weiskopf. He grinned impishly. "But it sounds like fun. Let's do it!"

"I found something at the lab I thought you might get a kick out of," said Dr. Wendy Wendell II, when she sat down to dinner with her family that evening.

"What is it?" asked her daughter, Wendy Wendell III.

"Finish your tofu and I'll tell you."

Wendy glared at her mother. "I think there's something in the constitution about cruel and unusual punishment," she muttered darkly.

"This isn't punishment, dear," said her father. "It's nutrition."

"I'm not sure that would hold up in court," said Wendy.

When it became clear that her mother was not going

to relent, Wendy's curiosity overcame her revulsion. "There," she said fifteen minutes later, choking down the last bite of the revolting stuff. "Now—what did you find?"

Dr. Wendell shifted her eyes from right to left, as if to make sure they were not being spied on. "A black glove!" she whispered conspiratorially.

Wendy's eyes widened.

"I found it in the hallway outside my office," continued her mother with a laugh. "It made me think of that spy you and your friends used to claim was here on Anza-bora Island."

She took the glove out of her pocket and handed it to Wendy.

"Thanks, Mom," said the Wonderchild, trying not to let her voice betray her excitement and her fear. "Gee, the gang sure will be interested to hear about this!"

Then she bolted from the table and headed for her terminal.

"I can't believe it," said Roger, when the gang had gathered at their headquarters in response to Wendy's emergency E-Mail. He was holding the black leather glove Wendy's mother had found and staring at it as if it had come from another planet.

"It could be just a coincidence," said Rachel. "I mean, it's not like Black Glove is the *only* person in the world who ever wore black gloves!"

"True," said Ray. "But given the climate on Anza-bora, how many people wear them *here?*"

Rachel sighed. "You've got a point."

"So you think he's come back?" asked Hap.

"Either that, or he never left," said Roger. "Remember Dr. Hwa figured that the boat that disappeared the night we found the transmitter meant Black Glove had fled the island. But what if our spy simply rigged that boat so it would sail away on auto-pilot, then blow up or sink a few miles out? He could still be here!"

"If it is a *he,*" said Trip. "It could well be a woman. You certainly can't tell from the size of the glove."

Roger turned the glove over in his hand. Aside from an odd bulge at the base of one of the fingers—and the fact that, as Ray had mentioned, no one would normally wear a glove in this climate—he could find nothing unusual about it.

The gang stayed up until late in the night talking about what the glove meant. In the end, all they could agree on was that they had to be more careful, more alert, than ever.

Close to morning the object of the gang's speculations slipped into the secret room beneath the computer center. Taking a seat at the terminal, Black Glove found a message announcing a piece of E-Mail that had been flagged by a special search program. The program had pulled the message from the hundreds sent between people on Anza-bora every day because it contained two key words: Black Glove.

It was, in fact, the E-Mail Wendy had sent to the gang after her mother had given her the black glove.

The spy's eyes widened in dismay. This had to be nipped in the bud!

Fingers flying, Black Glove began to type.

Wendy was sleeping when Black Glove's message arrived. That meant she was snoring, which meant her bedroom sounded like a small thunderstorm had just cracked loose inside it.

Competing with the noise of Wendy's snoring was Mr. Pumpkiss, her automated teddy bear. He was sitting on the Wonderchild's head, holding his toes and rocking back and forth while he sang "Melancholy Baby" at the top of his mechanical lungs.

The bear's morning concert had been triggered by a pair of light detectors Wendy had installed behind its eyes. When struck by enough light, they activated his singing. This made him a convenient alarm clock.

Wendy opened one bleary eye as the bear began a third chorus. She found herself staring at the bottom of a furry foot. "All right, Pumpkiss," she muttered. "I'm awake, I'm awake."

This was true, but only for a matter of seconds. Soon she was snoring again.

Blondie and Baby Pee Pants stood at the side of the bed, clamoring to be let up. Blondie was a twelve-inch tall plastic celebration of voluptuous womanhood, Baby Pee Pants a foul-mouthed baby doll. Like Mr. Pumpkiss, they had been programmed by Wendy to swing into action when the morning sun struck the photoreceptors hidden behind their glass eyes.

It was fortunate that they were mere automatons and not subject to hurt feelings, since waking their owner tended to be a thankless task. In fact, on a bad morning it could be downright dangerous.

"Captain Wendy," called the two dolls. "Get up, Captain Wendy. We're lonely!"

"Come to me, my melancholy baby," sang the bear, hiccuping on every fifth note.

"All right!" cried Wendy, sitting bolt upright. The bear fell into her lap, still singing. She pushed its nose, sending a signal to its electronic components that would end the concert.

She looked around her room and groaned. It was disgusting. Her parents had a robot that kept most of the house clean, of course. Unfortunately, its programming was not up to dealing with Wendy's room. Every time it came in to straighten up, it ended up rolling in helpless circles, muttering "Where do I begin? Where do I begin?"

Picking her way across the floor, Wendy located an old sweatshirt of her father's. She slipped it on, then sat down at her terminal and typed in a series of commands.

As far as Wendy was concerned, her access to the island's mainframe—to *ADAM,* she told herself, savoring the bit of classified information they had picked up from Dr. Weiskopf—was one of the few real benefits of living on this isolated stretch of sand.

However the horrifying message that now scrolled up on her monitor was enough to make her reconsider that idea.

7

Suspicions

"PUT DOWN THAT MONSTER AND EAT YOUR EGGS," said Mrs. Gammand impatiently. She was talking not to Ray, but to his father, Dr. Hugh Gammand.

Ray glanced up from his own eggs to see how his father would react to this command.

"Just a minute, dear," murmured Dr. Gammand. It was the only indication he gave that he had heard his wife's complaint. Without looking up, he continued to fiddle with "Thugwad the Gross," the hideous polystyrene creature beside his plate.

Ray was fairly certain his father actually had no idea that his breakfast was waiting for him. He smiled. While he had grown quite fond of his stepmother over the last two years, he did not always like the way she tried to impose her ideas on the household. His father had fiddled with monsters at the breakfast table for as long as Ray could remember. That was the way things were *supposed* to be.

"Is he for the new version of Gamma Ball, Dad?" asked Ray.

Dr. Gammand nodded and muttered something that sounded like "due yesterday."

Since the family made a great deal of money from the royalties Dr. Gammand received for his Gamma Ball games, Mrs. Gammand turned her attention to Ray. "What do you and your friends have planned for today?" she asked, trying to keep a pleasant tone in her voice.

Ray shrugged. "The same old stuff."

He wondered what she would say if he told her he was supposed to begin feeding information into an optical scanner designed to help them push the island's computer into awareness of its own existence.

The thought, slightly amusing, was followed by another that was deadly serious: *Just how interested would she be in that information?*

The idea that one of their parents could be the spy trying to leak information about Project Alpha was an unpleasant possibility each member of the A.I. Gang had to face in his or her own way. Most of the time Ray's tactic was simply not to think about it. But the fact was, his stepmother was a prime suspect, if for no other reason than that she had chosen to marry his father.

The thought made him sick. What if Elinor had only married his father because G.H.O.S.T. wanted her to spy on his work?

Ray shivered. Everyone in the gang wanted to believe Black Glove was one of the "strangers"—one of the scientists none of them was related to. But the hard fact was the person who planted the bug on Rachel's collar their first day on the island could have been any one of the adults at that orientation session.

What if it's Dr. Weiskopf? thought Ray suddenly. *Maybe this whole Euterpe thing is just a plot to set up a new method for getting information off the island.*

The thought depressed him. He didn't want to believe Dr. Weiskopf was capable of such a thing.

Be reasonable, he ordered himself. *No one would go to all the trouble it took to create Euterpe just to set up a way to send information to a bunch of spies.*

The thought made him feel better. But the seed of suspicion had been planted. He knew from experience it would be impossible to eliminate it completely.

Ray's thoughts were interrupted by a cry of dismay from his father. Thugwad had malfunctioned; the little monster was sitting in the middle of Dr. Gammand's plate, pounding on the fried eggs. The yolks were spattering in all directions, and several bright yellow spots now decorated Dr. Gammand's formerly white lab coat.

"Thugwad, you die!" cried the scientist. Snatching up his spoon, he smacked the dripping creature on top of its head.

Thugwad began beeping frantically.

Mrs. Gammand broke into helpless laughter. "Hugh, leave that poor creature alone!" she cried when she could catch her breath. "If you hadn't been fiddling with him at the table, this never would have happened!"

Dr. Gammand looked up in surprise. Thugwad fell over, landing on the toast, then began to twitch.

"Now look what you've done," said Mrs. Gammand severely. "He's got butter all over his sensors. Go clean him up."

"Yes, dear," said Dr. Gammand meekly. He scooped Thugwad into his hand and stood to leave the table.

Ray looked up in chagrin. It wasn't easy having a father who topped seven feet when you were barely pushing five yourself. But Dr. Gammand's height had turned out to have an unexpected benefit: It had cleared him of any suspicion that he might be Black Glove. The one time the gang had caught a glimpse of their foe, the spy had run under a pipe that was located five feet and seven inches above the floor— and done it without ducking.

Remembering that, Ray stole a glance at his stepmother.

She was only three inches taller than he was.

Plenty short enough to have cleared that pipe.

"Do you think we've bitten off more than we can chew?" asked Rachel Phillips.

"A fine question for you to ask!" said Roger. "Who was it that within the space of an hour decided we should both capture one of Brody's robots and build a rocket for Dr. Weiskopf's musical one?"

The twins were walking to the gang's headquarters. It was a beautiful morning on Anza-bora, and sunshine was streaming all around them. Not far away they could hear the roll of the breakers on the shore. The smell of the ocean filled the air.

"Let's take the day off and do nothing!" said Rachel.

"Idle hands are the devil's playground," said a metallic voice from the bag Rachel carried at her side.

"Shut up, Paracelsus," said Rachel, automatically uttering the cue to turn off the bronze head's ability to speak.

To her surprise, rather than falling silent the head cried, "Abuse! That's all I get from morning to night. It's enough to give me a headache—which is pretty serious, when you consider how I'm built!"

Rachel glared at her twin, who was whistling nonchalantly as he gazed out toward the ocean. "Roger, if you've changed the shut-off code . . ."

Roger looked astonished at the menacing tone in her voice. "It still turns him off," he said, his voice dripping with innocence. "I just thought he should have a chance to express an opinion before he was put out of commission."

"I think someone's going to put *you* out of commission if you're not careful, Roger," said Trip Davis, walking up behind them. "If I were a fortune-teller, I'd say you should be very watchful today. I see an angry redhead in your future."

Rachel glanced up at Trip. "Thank goodness you're here," she said. "Now I have someone sane to talk to."

Roger made a face at her.

"Cool it, guys," warned Trip. "Joggers coming." He

squinted into the distance. "I can't quite make out who they are."

"It's Dr. Ling and Dr. Fontana," said Rachel, more because she knew that the two female scientists were jogging partners than because she could make out their features.

"Good news at last!" cried Roger.

Rachel scowled. Among the males of the A.I. Gang, it was generally agreed that of all the scenic spots on Anza-bora Island, the most beautiful at any given moment was wherever the raven-haired Dr. Bai' Ling happened to be.

"Hi, kids!" said Dr. Fontana as she and Dr. Ling came puffing toward them. "What are you up to today?"

The women jogged in place as they waited for an answer.

"Not much," said Roger with a shrug. "We're going to install an optical scanner on the computer, figure out how to catch one of Brody's security robots, and then begin designing a major communications satellite."

It was all Trip could do to keep from jabbing Roger in the ribs.

"Well, at least you won't be bored," said Dr. Ling with a chuckle. She was wearing a visor, T-shirt, and shorts; her shoulder-length ebony hair glistened in the sunlight.

"Is that Paracelsus?" asked Dr. Fontana, indicating the bag that Rachel was carrying.

"Yes!" cried Paracelsus. "Thank God you found me! I've been kidnapped by gypsies!"

"Well, that answers that question," said Dr. Fontana with a smile. Her specialty was trying to make machines express themselves more clearly in human language, and she had been very impressed the first time she had seen Paracelsus in action. Now she never failed to ask about him when she ran into the twins.

"We'd better get moving if we're going to get our five miles in," puffed Dr. Ling. "See you kids later."

With that, the two women began running down the road. Trip and Roger watched until they were out of sight.

"You two are disgusting," said Rachel, shaking her head. "And I thought you told me Paracelsus's shut-off code still worked."

"It does," said Roger. "But I also put in a key so he would boot up if someone asked about him."

Rachel sighed and turned to Trip. "How would you like to let Roger be *your* brother for a week or so?" she asked. "I'd like to try being an only child for a while."

Hap Swenson squeezed a tiny drop of oil into the hole in Rin Tin Stainless Steel's belly, then glanced at his watch. He wished the others would get here. He was eager to get started for the day.

More than that, he wanted to tell them about the strange thing he had seen that morning.

He put the mechanical dog back onto its feet and walked to the computer console.

"Good morning, Hap," said Sherlock, when he had

punched in his identification code. "How are you today?"

Hap smiled. Though he has been skeptical when Roger had suggested that they give their terminal a British accent, it really did make the machine seem more real somehow; friendly, almost.

I wonder if it really will be friendly if it ever becomes truly conscious? thought Hap.

It wasn't the first time Hap had fretted about what success for the project would actually mean, not only for them, but for the rest of the world. He wondered if his own father even knew the real purpose of the Anza-bora Island project. The gang had figured it out from clues the others had picked up from their parents, who were actively working on the project. But Mr. Swenson was only here to keep the island's machines running. So he might never have been informed of the project's true goal.

Hap frowned. Even though his father had explained several times why they had not left with the others when the Air Force pulled out, it still seemed strange.

Like the rest of the gang, Hap was unwilling to believe that one of his parents might actually be Black Glove. But each of them had had a least one parent at that orientation meeting. So each of them, himself included, had at least one parent who was open to suspicion.

Hap's gloomy thoughts were interrupted by Wendy Wendell storming into the room. She was sputtering like a power cable that had fallen into a mud puddle.

"Have I got news for you guys!" she cried.

8

The Trap

"SEND THE MEN IN, SERGEANT BRODY," SAID BRIDGET McGrory, speaking into the intercom on her desk. "But let's keep this short, all right?"

She snapped off the intercom, then sighed. Brody's insistence on doing everything precisely by the book would drive her out of her mind yet.

Dr. Hwa stepped out of his office. Bridget went to his side. Together they watched as Sergeant Brody and his eight new guards filed into the room.

Ramon Korbuscek was third in line.

Those two would make good bookends, thought Korbuscek as he walked past the observers.

Indeed, with their short, jet-black hair and diminutive stature (neither stood more than a few inches above five feet) Dr. Hwa and Bridget McGrory did look like a matched set. Most of the island staff felt that they made a good pair in more ways than one. The feisty Irishwoman was notorious for shielding her softhearted boss from people who wanted too much of his time. Dr. Hwa, in turn, seemed to be the only person who could keep McGrory from removing someone's head once her temper had been aroused.

"Staff Sergeant Brody reporting, sir," said Brody, snapping off a salute.

Dr. Hwa gave him a gentle nod in return.

Korbuscek's gaze circled the room, taking in every detail. If he had to make a midnight visit it would be helpful to know the location of the desks, the chairs, the wall sockets, even the wastebasket.

Moreover, he could discern a great deal about someone's personality by the way he or she kept a room. This woman McGrory, for instance, was highly efficient and intolerant of intrusions. Comfort for visitors was almost nonexistent. Yet there were touches—the flower on her desk, the green silk scarf on the coatrack—that spoke of a softer side. That, too, was good to know.

The spy's brow furrowed momentarily. Other signs, even more subtle, indicated something else, something more interesting: This woman was keeping a secret.

Korbuscek's brain began to race. What was going on here?

While trying to analyze McGrory, Korbuscek was also listening to Dr. Hwa's brief remarks about the work being done on the island. Suddenly he felt a surge of excitement—no sign of which was allowed to reach his face. He had been sent to Anza-bora Island because the government that hired him was interested in a robot called Euterpe. After months of spying on the scientist who was making the robot, their operatives had temporarily lost track of him. Considerable effort had finally turned up the information that Dr. Leonard Weiskopf had moved to Anza-bora Island under "mysterious circumstances."

Now that government wanted to know what he was up to.

Actually, they wanted more than that. If Weiskopf was still working on his robot, they wanted a few "changes" made.

That was fine with Korbuscek. He would do exactly as his employers desired. But Dr. Hwa's speech, oblique as it was, confirmed what the spy had already begun to suspect. Whatever was being created on Anza-bora Island, it was bigger—much, *much* bigger—than the people who hired him had even begun to guess.

That meant information—information that could be sold to the highest bidder.

Looking at his face, no one could possibly have understood how happy that thought made Ramon Korbuscek.

From his position at the computer Hap looked up at the sputtering Wendy. "What guys? I'm the only one here."

Wendy scowled. "This is important. Where are they?"

"I don't have the slightest idea." Hap paused, then added tartly, "You don't have to wait for them to tell *me*, you know."

Wendy smacked her palm against her forehead. "Duh!" she said. "Sorry." Then, talking so fast she could barely keep her words straight, she spilled out the story of Black Glove's warning message.

Hap turned pale. But his response was interrupted by a commotion at the door as Roger, Rachel, and Trip came piling into the room. A moment later Ray, clutching his beloved basketball, came stumbling in as well.

"What happened to you two?" asked Roger, when he saw the expression on Hap and Wendy's faces. "You look like you just saw a ghost."

"Not saw," said Wendy. "Heard from. Black Glove left a message on my computer this morning."

It was impossible for her to speak above the babble that erupted at this statement.

"All right, everybody shut up!" shouted Roger finally. When the gang fell silent, he turned to Wendy and said, "Do you have the message?"

She snorted in disgust. "It disappeared, just as you would expect. But it also burned itself into my brain. I feel like Rachel; I can repeat the thing by heart."

"Go ahead," said Roger.

Wendy cleared her throat, and began to recite:

Miss Wendell:

This is a warning.

The people I work for have suffered enough from your foolish interference. You and your friends will stay out of my affairs, or suffer the consequences.

If you question this, let me review a few points for you.

You know I exist, but you cannot convince anyone else that I am real. Even worse, you have no idea who I am. You do not know where to find me, or how to fight me.

I, on the other hand, know who each of you is. I can contact you by computer anytime I wish. Much of the time I can see what you are doing. At times I can even hear you.

I have power. You do not.

Until today, I have been taking it easy on you. But I am not playing any longer. Cease to bother me, or be prepared to suffer the consequences.

Remember: I am watching.

And I may watch one of you die.

—Black Glove

When the Wonderchild was done a heavy silence hung over the group.

"He's bluffing," said Roger at last.

"Or she," said Wendy. "And I don't know if I agree with you. We're playing in the big leagues here."

"Agreed," said Roger. "But if the main thing on Black Glove's mind is getting information off the island, then he or she can't do much unless there's information *to* get off. If something happened to one of us, even accidentally, it would blow this place apart. The least that would happen is that things would slow down.

More likely it would actually cause some of the scientists to leave. I'm pretty sure Dad would want to get away from here if anything happened to Rachel or me."

"I think my folks would feel the same," said Trip. "And that could bring the project to a standstill. These people are the best in the country—in the world, most of them. It wouldn't be easy to replace them."

"My point exactly," said Roger. "I just don't think Black Glove will want to take that chance."

"Great," said Hap. "That means if the enemy starts feeling cranky, I'll be number one on the hit parade, since *my* folks don't really make much difference to the success of the project."

"Maybe we should just drop the whole thing," said Rachel, who had been chewing on the back of her thumb.

"No," said Hap firmly. "We can't do that, either." He stood up and began pacing. "I've done a lot of thinking about this project lately. Frankly I'm not sure the thing is such a good idea to begin with; I get a little scared just thinking about what this computer might be able to do. But I doubt I could convince Dr. Hwa to call things off. So the odds are there really *is* going to be a computer that can think. If that's the case, I sure don't want it in the hands of G.H.O.S.T.! And since we can't get anyone else to take this seriously, that leaves it up to us. Risky? You bet. But I don't even want to think about the alternative."

"Then I'd say it's time to get busy," said Wendy. She pushed up the sleeves of her sweatshirt, then blinked and said, "What should we do first?"

"Finish the optical scanner?" suggested Trip.

"Already done!" said Hap. "I finished it last night. Would have had it done earlier, but I had to cobble up some substitutes for the parts that we couldn't get from the warehouse because of Brody's robots."

"I hate to say this, but those robots should probably be our first project," said Ray. "Until we handle that situation, we can be seriously slowed down any time we need a spare part."

"Don't forget Dr. Weiskopf's rocket," said Rachel. "We promised to build that, too."

"I don't know," said Roger. "It seems to me that's one project that *can* go on hold for the time being. We've got more important stuff to—" he paused, and a strange but familiar look appeared in his eyes. "Wait a minute! Stand back, everyone! I think I'm about to be brilliant!"

The rest of the gang looked at him nervously. Roger's brainstorms were known to be hazardous to other people's health.

"Oh, this is great!" he cried, looking at the ceiling. Then, turning his eyes back to the others, he said, "It's time we tracked down Black Glove and put a stop to this mess."

"But that's the purpose of Operation Sherlock," said Hap.

"I know," said Roger. "And it was a darn good idea."

"You're only saying that because you thought of it yourself," said Wendy.

"High self-esteem is essential to a happy life. Now

71

shut up and listen. Sherlock is supposed to crack the case and figure out who the enemy is. The problem is, we might all be dead before we get the program in shape to do that."

"I love an optimist," said Paracelsus.

"Shut up," hissed Rachel, "or I'll disconnect your power source."

"Abuse!" cried Paracelsus. "That's all it is. Abu-u-u—*awk!*"

An uneasy silence filled the room. The others turned toward Rachel, who had done exactly as she threatened and disconnected Paracelsus.

"Don't look at me like that!" she ordered, blushing. "It's not like I killed him. I'll turn him back on later."

"Machinicide," said Trip sadly. "The crime of the future is with us today."

"Oh, be quiet or I'll pull your plug, too! Roger, finish what you were saying."

"Thank you," said Roger as Trip shrank from Rachel in feigned horror. "The point I was trying to make was that we should consider switching tactics. Right now we're on the defensive. Black Glove acts, and we respond. Let's reverse the process."

"What are you suggesting?" asked Ray.

"I think we should set a trap for Black Glove. What's more, I think Dr. Weiskopf's rocket could be the perfect bait."

He waited for the noise to die down before he continued with his plan. "What's the one thing B.G. wants most in life?"

"Disregarding personal quirks, I'd say it's to get information off this island," replied Trip.

"Correctamundo! Now, since we recently succeeded in thoroughly screwing up his method for doing that, it's reasonable to assume he's a little desperate—especially given Brody's security crackdown. All right, let's imagine a perfect way to get secret information from here to somewhere else. How does a satellite sound? A satellite launched from this island and designed to circumvent the electronic shield that cuts us off from the rest of the world, since there should be no problem just sending information back and forth between Anza-bora and the satellite. Let me tell you, as soon as Black Glove finds out what we're up to, he—or she—is going to spot the possibilities immediately. A little fiddling with the system, maybe plant a special device in the rocket, and Bingo!—a new way to communicate with G.H.O.S.T.!"

"We can't take that kind of a chance with Euterpe!" cried Rachel.

"But don't you see? That's exactly what we *were* going to do! We just hadn't realized it. The only thing I'm suggesting is that instead of blindly letting Black Glove take advantage of what we build that we turn the tables and use it to take advantage of him. And frankly, Rachel, it's the only reason I can think of to take the time to build that rocket right now. If we use our brains, we can build two things at once: a rocket to launch Euterpe, and a trap to catch a spy."

9

The Brain Cell

TRIP AND RAY SAT IN DR. ARMAND MERCURY'S kitchen, watching him beat the living daylights out of a half dozen egg whites. After a while the portly scientist put down the bowl, peered inside, then dipped a stubby finger into the contents.

"This is going to be superb," he pronounced, licking the goo from his fingertip. "I hope you can stay and have some."

"What is it?" asked Ray.

"Right now? Nothing. When I am done? Ah, when I am done it will be a superb chocolate soufflé with Grand Marnier and fresh orange slices."

Looking at Dr. Mercury's rotund figure, Trip thought that the man had probably already had enough soufflés to last him a lifetime.

The scientist poured his concoction into a springform pan and carefully placed it in the oven.

"Actually, I'm making this for Dr. Remov. He's coming over when he's done at the Brain Cell. I'm sure he'd be glad to see you if you can stay."

"What's the Brain Cell?" asked Trip.

Dr. Mercury's eyes grew wide and he put his fingers to his full lips in mock chagrin. "Silly me!" he said, making a little snort. "It's the secret name for the central command center for Project Alpha. It's supposed to be classified—but unless you're like Stanley and believe in crackpot theories about Black Glove and G.H.O.S.T., I can't figure out what difference it makes." He winked at them. "Just don't tell anyone you heard it from me, all right?"

"You've got our word," said Trip.

"Well, that's a relief," said Dr. Mercury, putting his hand to his heart. Realizing that his fingers were covered with flour, he began wiping them on his lab coat, asking as he did, "So what is it that brings you two here? Despite my charm and wit, I have a feeling this is not merely a social visit."

Trip glanced at his partner. It was the Gamma Ray who had pointed out that until they got the matter of the security robots under control their other work could be stymied by lack of materials at any time. That was why they were here now, on what was, for them, a most unusual scrounging mission. Instead of scouring the warehouses, they were actually going to *ask* to borrow something. Trip felt almost as if they were breaking the rules of the game.

Unfortunately, with Brody's robots still in action, they had no choice.

When Ray didn't speak up, Trip finally said, "We're working on a little project, sir. We know you specialize in sound command systems, and we were wondering if we could borrow a pair of synthesizer guns."

Dr. Mercury's keen eyes seemed to burrow into Trip's skull. After a moment he pursed his lips and pressed his chubby hands together. "Do you know exactly what a synthesizer gun is?"

"Sure," said Ray. "Sound engineers use them to create precise tones for audio control systems. You can dial up virtually any form of sound wave and direct it at a target."

"And what what would you want something like that for?"

"We're working on a robot control system," replied Trip, remembering Roger's oft-repeated dictum that truth was the simplest disguise.

Dr. Mercury chuckled. "Sounds like an interesting project. Give me a minute, I'll see what I can dig up for you."

Trip's eyes followed the scientist as he waddled away from the table and disappeared into another room.

"He knows what we're up to!" he whispered. "I could see it in his face. And you know what that means."

Ray shrugged. "I guess it means he doesn't care if we screw up Brody's robots. Which could mean—"

"One of two things," interrupted Trip. "Either (a) Dr. Mercury is really Black Glove and wants the robots out of commission for reasons of his own, or else (b) he's like most of the rest of the people here and would be glad to see us make a monkey out of Brody."

Ray smiled. "Either way, we get what we need," he said. Then a troubled look replaced his smile. "He *is* short enough to be Black Glove."

Trip nodded. "I know. I've been trying not to think about it, because he's such a nice guy. But when you come right down to it, *all* the suspects seem pretty decent. The problem is, one of them isn't."

Ray shivered. "If he really is Black Glove we might be playing right into his hands."

"Here we are!" boomed Dr. Mercury, heaving himself back into the room. "I knew I had a couple of these things around here somewhere."

He held out a pair of the sound guns and gave the boys a big wink. "I want you to promise you'll make good use of these."

Then he began to chuckle.

"Well, that's the last of them," said Wendy, drawing the still warm stack of papers out of the machine. She pushed back one of her pigtails and passed the pile to Rachel.

"That thing is amazing," said Hap, referring to the state-of-the-art crystal-based printer Wendy had borrowed from her parents. It could churn out a five-hundred-page book in less than three minutes.

"The printer is okay," said Rachel. "It's Wendy's password program that's boggling my mind."

"Aw, shucks," said Wendy, batting her eyes. "Twarn't nothin', ma'am."

Secretly she was pleased by Rachel's praise—especially since the program had nearly turned out to be a total embarrassment. After assuring the others that she could easily tap into the mainframe's secret files, she had discovered that the computer's security system was more complex than she had suspected. For weeks the thing had blocked all her attempts to milk it for data. Cracking its security code had taken considerably more work than she had anticipated.

She suppressed a shiver. Given this morning's message from Black Glove, she had succeeded just in time.

Roger glanced through the stack of papers and let out a low whistle. "I think we're playing with fire this time, guys. If the adults ever find out we pulled this stuff out of the mainframe, we'll really be in the stew."

Rachel pressed one of the stickers she had been preparing onto a folder, labeling its contents. "Desperate times require desperate measures," she said primly. "By the way, here's Dad's file."

Roger took the sheaf of papers and began leafing through it.

They had created seventeen folders in all, one for each major suspect. Inside the folders were the hard-copy versions of the ultrasecret personnel files Wendy had called up from the computer.

"I didn't know Dr. Clark liked to water-ski," said Hap, flipping through one of the files. He tried to imagine the tall, chestnut-haired woman skimming across the water behind a powerboat, but the picture didn't make sense. He shook his head. "She seems too dignified for something like that."

Before anyone could answer, the door swung open, revealing two masked figures.

"All right, everybody!" shouted the taller one. "Hit the floor!"

"That means now," said the shorter one, pointing a strange-looking gun toward the center of the room.

Rachel's initial surge of fright was immediately replaced by one of righteous indignation. "If we weren't stuck in the middle of the Pacific Ocean, I'd call a rest home to come get you two," she said angrily.

The taller figure peeled off its mask to reveal the grinning face of Trip Davis. "Sorry," he said. "We couldn't help ourselves."

"Aren't these guns neat!" enthused Ray, waving his in the air.

"Neat," said Roger. "Now get your basketball and come here. We've got work to do."

"All right, all right," said Ray. "Don't get hyper. You'll have a heart attack and end up in the infirmary with Dr. Clark's icy fingers wrapped around your wrist."

"Infirmary!" cried Hap. "That's what I wanted to

tell you guys. With everything that's been going on today, it slipped my mind."

"Care to explain what you're babbling about?" asked Roger.

"Well, to begin with, I got up early this morning."

"Don't worry," said Wendy sympathetically. "Another year or two and we'll have you on civilized hours."

"Usually I take kind of a cross-country path to get here," continued Hap, ignoring the interruption. "As I was cutting past the infirmary this morning, I saw a guy letting himself into it."

Ray shrugged. "So maybe he needed a Band-Aid."

"Could be. Like I said, it might not mean anything. But a few things about it bothered me. First, the building isn't supposed to be open at that time. Second, the way he was looking around gave me the impression he had no business being there. Third, while I couldn't really study him, he didn't look like anybody I've ever seen here before."

"Plasmagacious!" cried Wendy. "Another mystery! Just what we didn't need."

"It was probably one of Brody's new men," said Roger. "He was supposed to have a whole crew on the last plane. Those guys probably have access to every building on the island."

Hap shook his head. "What you're saying makes sense. But something about the way this guy moved made me suspicious. I don't think he even saw me, and he was still acting spooky."

"Okay, we'll put it in the Sherlock files," said

Roger. "Right now, Operation Scramble has to be our main priority. If we're going to capture one of Brody's robots, we'd better get busy. Come on, let's see if we can figure out how to use these sound guns."

An hour later they had come to the painful conclusion that two guns would be insufficient; they needed four to do the job.

"Could we build a couple?" asked Trip uncertainly.

"Maybe, if we had two months," said Ray gloomily.

"That, and free access to the warehouse so we could get spare parts," said Wendy. "But that's the whole point of this project to begin with."

"Do you need four guns, or just four sound sources?" asked Hap.

Roger looked up from his pacing. "Why?"

"Well, I think I might be able to make some extensions for these things."

"What do you mean?" asked Rachel.

"I think I could wire an extra speaker to run off of each of these guns. Would that do what we need? You couldn't make different sounds, of course. But from the way you were talking earlier, I got the impression that what we really needed was four different *sources* for the sounds."

"Hap, you are the official recipient of today's genius award," said Roger. "Wire away!"

It took the rest of that day, and most of the next, to do the wiring. While Hap was working on it, the others were doing something nearly as difficult: arranging things so that everyone would be free to carry out their plans that night.

It was well past midnight when the gang reunited at the headquarters. Taking three dune buggies, they drove to Warehouse Two, where they separated according to plan.

It wasn't until Rachel was actually standing at the door of the warehouse that she began to wonder if this expedition was such a good idea after all. Lifting her hand to her face, she found that she was trembling. She was glad that the luck of the draw had teamed her up with Hap. She found his quiet competence deeply reassuring.

"Come on," he whispered now. "Let's get into position."

They had left their shoes in the dune buggy. Sliding over the warehouse floor on stockinged feet, they moved in near perfect silence.

"There," whispered Hap. "That's our spot."

They took their positions. After a moment Rachel stole a glance at the husky blond crouching beside her. The fact that she liked Hap so much was beginning to bother her. She had more important things to spend her time on than thinking about boys! Yet she found Hap crossing her mind more times a day than she wanted to admit.

All right, Phillips, she told herself sternly. *Get your mind on target. If that robot comes rolling into view while you're mooning around over Golden Boy here, you may be one sorry cookie. Pay attention!*

She wondered how Roger was making out. He and Trip were hidden in the shadows directly across from them, waiting for Ray to make his move.

Shoeless like the others, the Gamma Ray slid into the open space between his friends. So far they had managed to move silently enough not to attract any of the robots.

Now that they were all in place, the plan was for that to change.

Why me? thought Ray, looking around nervously.

Straining his eyes, he spotted Roger in the shadows.

The red-haired twin flashed him a thumbs-up sign.

Ray sighed. No sense in putting it off any longer. Slamming his basketball against the floor, he began dribbling for all he was worth.

It wouldn't take long, he was sure, before Death-monger heard him.

10

Robo-Disaster

ALL RIGHT, THOUGHT RAY, PEERING ABOUT. *WHERE'S the stupid robot?*

He stopped dribbling and turned in a slow circle.

No sign of the thing.

He threw the ball against the floor again.

The loud *bounce!* echoed through the empty warehouse.

Still no sign of the robot.

Ray shrugged and began a high-speed dribble, making tight circles in the center of the warehouse. If he had to attract the robot's attention, he might as well get a little practice in while he was at it. He launched himself into the air to slam the ball through an imaginary hoop.

Ray was well aware that as a general rule what goes up must come down. To his dismay, he now found himself disobeying that ancient dictum. He had gone up—but he wasn't coming down.

The floor! he thought desperately. *Where's the floor?*

"Got you!" rasped a terrifying metallic voice, mere inches from his ear. At the same instant Ray became aware of the fierce metal pincers digging into his sides.

Deathmonger had snatched him in midleap!

Ray let out a bloodcurdling shriek. Suddenly it seemed as if the whole world were exploding. A cacophony broke loose in the warehouse. The robot began to spin in a circle, buzzing furiously. Through his haze of fear, Ray could hear Roger issuing orders: "Trip, move right. Hap, off to the left!"

Ray tried to make sense of what was happening, but the robot was whirling so fast he couldn't focus on anything.

Then, suddenly, the metallic monster dropped him. He slammed into the floor, the air rushing out of his lungs as if someone had stepped on him.

"More frequency modulation," cried Roger. "Especially at the upper end!"

"Ray!" shouted Trip. "Get out of there!"

Too dizzy to walk, Ray pushed himself to his hands and knees and began crawling from the spot where Deathmonger had dropped him. He hadn't gone more than three feet when he heard something crash to the floor behind him.

"Got it!" cried Roger. "Wrap those coils around it. Fast! Wendy, get in here!"

Ray opened his eyes and tried to move again. He was staring at a pile of wooden boxes. Carefully turning around (how could the floor be moving so fast when he was on his hands and knees?), he saw the robot lying on its back, its wheels spinning helplessly in the air. Trip and Hap were wrapping coils of high-tension spring wire around it while Roger and Rachel held it at bay with the sound guns.

A dune buggy rolled into the warehouse and pulled to a stop beside the robot. "Sorry," said Wendy. "I had to move a stack of boxes to get over here." She looked at Deathmonger. "How can something mechanical look so mad? Is it secure yet?"

"Barely," said Trip, stepping away from it. "If we had more wire, I'd keep wrapping. As it is, I'd suggest we get moving."

"Then let's get it on board," said Wendy.

Hap, Roger, Rachel, and Trip moved toward the fallen robot. Positioning themselves two on a side, they tried to lift it.

To their horrified surprise, they were unable to budge the thing. It was far heavier than they had suspected.

Wendy joined them, but it made no difference.

Ray tried to stagger over to help, too, but was still so dizzy from the robot's whirling that he fell back down.

Roger looked around desperately for something—anything—to help them move the mechanized monster.

Ray was watching the ceiling whirl when he noticed a network of track overhead. It took him a moment to make sense of what he was seeing. When it clicked into place, he rolled over, pushed himself to his knees, and cried, "Skyhook! Skyhook!"

Roger looked up. "Ray, if you were on salary, I'd give you a raise."

"I think I saw the controls when we came in," said Wendy. "They were over that way."

"Let's move!" yelled Roger. He grabbed the Wonderchild by the hand and together they dashed in the direction Wendy had indicated.

Trip helped Ray to his feet. "I hope we get out of here soon," he said nervously. "I doubt even Roger can talk us out of this one if we get caught."

At that moment a huge hook swung down from the ceiling.

"We may just make it," said Ray. "Get that hook into the bindings, you guys."

Rachel and Hap grabbed the hook. But when they approached the robot, it let out a sudden bellow.

They jumped back nervously.

"Oh, for heaven's sake!" exclaimed Ray, who was still feeling embarrassed that he hadn't been able to help with the attempts to lift the thing. Shaking himself free of Trip's supporting arm, he grabbed the hook from Rachel. Moving quickly despite his grogginess, he slipped the end of it under the wire the others had used to bind the robot.

"I guess familiarity does breed contempt," he said, giving the chain attached to the hook a hearty tug. "I can't take this thing too seriously now that it's flat on its back."

Not taking it seriously was a mistake. Even as Roger responded to Ray's signal by retracting the chain, a tentaclelike extension lashed out from the robot and wrapped itself around Ray's waist.

Pulled by the hook, the robot rose into the air. Shouting and struggling, the Gamma Ray rose with it.

Ramon Korbuscek slipped quietly through the shadows surrounding a darkened house near the center of Anza-bora Island.

A tingle of pleasure rippled over the spy's skin. He always enjoyed the thrill of risk that accompanied even a simple break-in. With the unexpected target he had found for tonight, the excitement he felt now was like a small fire.

He crouched beside a low bush to check the house again.

No sign of life. Indeed, if the lights were any indication, the occupant had turned in two hours ago, shortly after midnight. It would be reasonable to expect him to be asleep by now.

That didn't mean he would be, of course. Korbuscek was well aware of the dangers of assumption. The old man who lived in this house might be lying awake with insomnia; he might be in the bathroom; he might even be sitting up with only a tiny reading light on, absorbed in one of those paperback thrillers Korbuscek knew he enjoyed so much.

You could never be sure.

Korbuscek patted his vest. He liked to feel the rows of pockets filled with the most sophisticated tricks the wizards of electronics, chemistry, and biology had been able to dream up.

His hand lingered on a small plastic vial. If broken, it would release a gas that would throw anyone within a ten-foot radius into a deep and peaceful slumber. Better yet, it would cause them to totally forget whatever had happened just before they passed out.

Reassured of the gas, Korbuscek tapped the side of his nose to make certain his filters were in place. (He always wore nasal filters on a mission like this. After all, his vest held more than a dozen different gasses, some deadly enough to drop a herd of elephants.)

Enough waiting! he chided himself. *Time to start.*

Moving like a shadow, the spy crossed the lawn and approached the back door of the house.

A smile flickered over his lips as he stepped onto the porch. He had been looking forward to this operation since he turned up the listing of island personnel during his little "visit" to the clinic that morning. The smile changed to a frown when he recalled the blond boy who had spotted him as he was leaving the infirmary. He had already picked up enough gossip to know that the kids here might be a problem.

Still, the foray had been worth it. With their detailed medical records, clinics were always a prime source for useful information on the staff of a given place—yielding everything from names and ages to such helpful tidbits as allergies and medical weaknesses that could be used to put a person out of commission when necessary.

Though Korbuscek had been raiding clinics for years, never had one yielded a piece of information that surprised or delighted him as what he had found that morning: the name of the fierce old enemy who was now part of Project Alpha.

Dr. Weiskopf and his robot could wait for a little while.

At the moment, Ramon Korbuscek wanted to find out what Dr. Stanley Remov was up to these days.

Staff Sergeant Artemus P. Brody sat up in his bed and groaned. How long had that beeper been sounding?

Brody blinked. The "beeper" was the alarm that indicated one of the guard robots had cornered something! If it was those damn kids again . . .

Growling to himself, Brody flung his legs over the side of the bed and began to pull on his pants. He had a feeling this was not a *real* emergency. If he was right, someone was going to be very, very sorry.

Stumbling into the main room of his quarters, he punched a button on the wall and snapped, "Peters! There's trouble with one of the robots. Meet me in the staff room. *Now!*"

Brody stomped out of his quarters. When he reached the staff room, he noticed a light flashing on the chart posted on the back wall. He squinted at it and frowned. Warehouse Two again. It *had* to be the kids.

Brody pivoted at the sound of someone entering the room.

"What's up, chief?" asked Corporal Peters, stifling a yawn.

Before Brody could answer, the beeper's tone changed. Brody smiled and took a deep breath. The robot was signaling that it had made a capture.

That meant he could slow down just a bit. Let whoever had disturbed his sleep suffer for a while. He would get there soon enough.

"Oh, Rogerrrr!" called Wendy. "We've got a problem."

"Get me outta here!" bellowed the Gamma Ray, squirming wildly as he tried to break free from the robot's grip.

"Stop struggling!" cried Rachel. "If you *do* get loose, you might kill yourself."

This seemed like a real possibility, since both Ray and the robot were suspended some fifteen feet above the warehouse floor. The robot, dangling from the "skyhook," swung lazily back and forth, like a yo-yo twisting at the end of its string.

Roger came running from where he had been operating the skyhook controls. When he saw Ray, he groaned in despair.

"We've got to get him free from that robot," said Trip.

"There's no time," replied Roger. "If we're not out of here about five seconds ago, we're dead meat."

He started back toward the control panel. "Trip, get the dune buggy in position underneath them. The rest of you stand ready to center Ray and his friend there over it. Wendy, station yourself where you can keep an eye on Ray and still talk to me so you can guide me. Let's *move,* guys! And stop kicking, Ray. You'll only make things worse."

By this time he had reached the control panel. He threw a switch, and the skyhook began to descend, dropping Deathmonger and Ray toward the back of the dune buggy.

"Steady, Roger!" yelled Wendy, who was standing at the end of a row of crates, in a spot from which she could see both the dune buggy and the control panel. "A little to the right. No, too much! *Too much!* Bring it back a bit!"

The robot's eyes were flashing, its wheels spinning at a furious pace. Suddenly it began to speak again. "Death to the intruders!" it snarled. "Death to the intruders!"

"Oh, God! Get me out of here quick!" yelled Ray.

By now the Ray-robot combo was suspended only three feet above the dune buggy. Stretching onto their toes, Hap and Rachel tried to stop it from swaying.

"Quit struggling, Ray!" snapped Rachel. "It makes it harder to keep you in position!"

"All right, bring them down!" yelled Wendy when she saw that the others had the combo in position. "A little farther ... a little farther ... Bull's-eye!"

Roger came barreling around the corner as Rachel

disconnected the skyhook. Ray and his captor were wedged cozily into the backseat of the dune buggy.

"All right, let's get out of here!" yelled Roger.

"Aren't you going to get me loose first?"

"No time, buddy!" replied Roger, jumping onto the rear bumper. "Brody will be here any second. Let's get a move on, you guys. Floor it, Trip!"

The dune buggy, loaded with all six kids plus the robot, zoomed forward.

"Hey, watch it!" cried Hap as Trip came close to sideswiping a towering stack of crates. He wasn't worried about knocking the things over; he was hanging on the outside edge of the buggy, and afraid he would get scraped off himself.

Careening down an alley made of boxes, taking the corner on two wheels, Trip shot out of the warehouse and into the night.

"To your own buggies!" cried Roger. Jumping off the bumper, he scrambled behind the wheel of his own vehicle. Wendy tumbled in beside him, shoving Roger over so she could take the wheel. Rachel and Hap raced across the sand to the buggy they had driven to the warehouse.

Without waiting for the others, Trip headed for the road. He bounced the sturdy little vehicle onto the pavement, then straight across and off the other side. No sense in making himself easy to find by sticking to the main path.

"Let's split up," said Roger as Wendy pulled their

buggy up next to the one Hap was driving. "It'll make it that much harder for them to trail us."

"Good idea," said Hap. "See you at the cavern?"

"See you at the cavern."

The two dune buggies sped silently in opposite directions.

Sergeant Brody arrived at Warehouse Two a few seconds later. He found the door wide open. His prize security robot Deathmonger had vanished without a trace.

Ramon Korbuscek shifted uneasily in the darkened house. Was that a sound in the room above him?

He held his breath and listened.

Nothing.

Must be my nerves.

The idea disturbed him. He had a reputation throughout the intelligence community for being cool under the most trying circumstances. The fact that this house was occupied by his oldest, bitterest enemy was no excuse for getting jumpy.

He forced himself to take a few deep breaths, then returned to the papers he had been photographing. Perhaps his nervousness was caused not by memories of what Remov could do, but by the incredible potential of what he, Korbuscek, had stumbled into.

Good old computer-wizard Remov. When I told him I was going to get rich on what I learned from him, I had no idea it would be this way!

Korbuscek finished photographing the papers and

tucked them back into the file, which he had found precisely where he had expected.

It had all been so easy he almost felt let down as he slipped out of the house.

That feeling vanished when a dark figure jumped him from behind.

Ray Gammand was convinced that the ride to the cavern was taking twice as long as it ever had before. As the dune buggy bounced along he found himself aching in at least fifteen different places—and he had a feeling there were others he wasn't even aware of yet.

To make matters worse, the stupid robot that held him in its clutches wouldn't shut up. By the time they reached the cavern, Ray was certain if he heard "Death to the intruders!" one more time he was going to lose his mind. When he thought about it further, he decided he must have lost his mind already. Otherwise he would never have gotten into this mess!

He waited impatiently as Trip maneuvered the dune buggy as close as possible to the mouth of the cavern.

They had decided to bring the robot here because they knew odds were good that the thing had some kind of tracking device attached to it—which meant if they took it back to their headquarters, Brody and his men would be knocking at their door before dawn.

It was Hap who had suggested the cavern. "Even if they manage to track us there, they probably won't be able to find the way in," he had claimed.

That made sense; as far as the gang knew, no one else on the island was even aware of the cavern.

Trip scrambled out of the front seat and hurried around to the back of the dune buggy. "How are you doing, buddy?" he asked.

"Terrible!" growled Ray.

Just then Roger and Wendy drove up. "Let's get inside," said Roger. "Then we can figure out how to spring Ray without worrying about Brody showing up."

"You're going to owe me a lot of favors for this one, Roger," said Ray.

Trip was already pulling at the pile of brush and rocks they had created to hide the entrance to the cavern. "Give me a hand, will you?" he yelled. "We haven't got all night!"

Roger and Wendy were at his side in an instant. The three worked in silence until the area was clear.

"That's it!" said Trip, as he dragged away the last of the big stones. Wiping the sweat from his brow, he headed back to the dune buggy. "It won't be long now, Ray," he said as he slipped behind the wheel.

"Roger!" called Wendy. "Are you coming?"

"Huh? Oh sure, sure. Be right there."

But the redhead continued to stand at the mouth of the cave, staring back in the direction they had come. He was searching for a pair of headlights—or anything to indicate the approach of another vehicle.

Search as he might, he saw nothing.

11

Rachel and Hap

RAMON KORBUSCEK AND DR. STANLEY REMOV rolled over and over in the dirt, pummeling each other with their fists.

The fight was strangely silent. Neither man cried out for help, neither cried out in anger. The only sounds were the ones they made scrabbling against the soil and the occasional thud of a well-aimed punch.

For several minutes the battle was nearly even. Then Korbuscek landed a solid blow on Dr. Remov's jaw. The older man fell back, his head striking the ground heavily.

Pressing his advantage, Korbuscek hit him again, and yet again.

Dr. Remov's struggles grew weaker.

Then a strange thing happened. Korbuscek drew back his fist to deliver what would surely have been the final blow. Yet at a whispered word from Dr.

Remov, he let his fist drop. Crying out in terror, he scrambled from his fallen opponent and ran into the darkness as if the hounds of hell were at his heels.

Dr. Remov lay very still for several minutes.

Then he began to chuckle.

When he tried to move, however, his chuckles turned to groans. Slowly, each move an agony, he began dragging himself toward his house.

He collapsed before he was halfway there.

If Rachel and Hap's dune buggy had been making any noise at all, they would never have found Dr. Remov. Only the silence of the electric motor (and the fact that they were moving at little better than a crawl) made it possible for the scientist's low moans to reach their ears.

Rachel was the first to hear him—largely because Hap was focusing so thoroughly on the road. The reason for his intensity was simple: He was driving without lights, to avoid attracting attention. But he was so fixed on what he was doing that when Rachel grabbed his arm and hissed, "What was that?" he nearly spun them off the road.

"Don't do that!" he yelled. Then, remembering that they were trying to be silent, he lowered his voice. "What was *what?* I didn't hear anything."

"Shhh!" said Rachel. "Be quiet and listen."

Hap obeyed, slowing the buggy even further to do so.

"There. Didn't you hear it? Stop the buggy!"

"I still don't hear anything," grumbled Hap as he applied the brake again. "I hope you know what you're doing!"

They sat in silence for a moment, both straining their ears. This time Hap heard the moan, too. "It came from over there!" he whispered.

"Right!" agreed Rachel. "It sounds like someone in trouble. Let's go!"

Hap grabbed her arm as she started to scramble out of the dune buggy. "Take it easy. We don't want to get caught out here at this time of night. Let's make sure this is really an emergency before we go getting ourselves in trouble."

Rachel hesitated, then nodded. The movement was barely visible in the starlight. Moving quietly, they worked their way toward the source of the sound. After their second tumble, they clasped hands to keep each other from falling.

"There it is again," whispered Rachel, trying to concentrate on the business at hand and not the nearness of Hap. "It *is* someone in trouble!"

Hap switched on the flashlight he had pulled from the buggy and pointed it in the direction of the sound.

Rachel clutched his arm and cried out in horror.

"Roger, will you get in here?" cried Trip impatiently. "I need your help!"

"Yeah, yeah," said Roger. "Be right there." He took one last look in the direction where Wendy had

99

just disappeared in her dune buggy to search for Rachel and Hap, then turned and hurried into the cavern.

Ray was still trapped in Deathmonger's clutches.

"Careful!" said Trip as Roger began to tug at one of the metal tentacles. "We don't want to damage it."

"I don't care if you *destroy* it!" said Ray. "JUST GET ME OUT OF HERE!"

"Will you both be quiet!" snapped Roger as he struggled to disengage Ray from the robot's tenacious grip.

Everyone fell silent—except for the robot, which continued to chant, "Death to the intruders!" in its crude, rasping voice. Trip didn't mind the reprimand, since he knew what had caused it. In the time he had known Roger, he had rarely seen him get angry, no matter how difficult the task they faced. But right now they were all on edge with worry about Rachel and Hap, and none more so than Rachel's twin.

In a way Trip envied Wendy, who had gone out to look for the strays. Action was always better than waiting, even if you *were* busy with another important task.

"There's got to be a service panel here somewhere," said Roger in exasperation. "Trip, move that light to the right."

Trip picked up the lantern. Stalactites and stalagmites glimmered in its stray beams, great rocky fangs that thrust from the floor and ceiling of the cavern. As Trip moved the light in the direction Roger had indicated, the patches of shadow it cast flowed across the stone walls like giant fingers groping for a lost dream. Trip smiled. For as long as he could remember, he had loved caves. He found them enthralling, always felt they might somehow lead you to some deep and ancient secret in the heart of the earth. Next to the ones about flying, his favorite dreams were always about caves.

"Found it!" crowed Roger, prying up a flap of metal on the side of the robot's head. "Now we should get somewhere!"

He began poking around in the robot's skull.

"Death to the intruders!" it roared. "Death to the death to the deathtothe tothe to ghliiikn . . ."

"Well, that takes care of that," said Trip.

"A lucky guess," said Roger.

"See if you can make another one, will you?" moaned Ray. "If you don't get me out of here soon I'll still have black and blue marks by the time I'm old enough to vote!"

Roger squinted into the control box. The tip of his tongue was sticking out from between his lips, as it always did when he needed to concentrate and couldn't rub his fingers together. "Here goes nothing," he said, poking at a button with his screwdriver.

Immediately the robot began to tighten the tentacle it had wrapped around Ray's waist.

"Turn it off!" screamed the captive. "It's killing me!"

Roger worked desperately at the button. It wouldn't come back out.

"*It's breaking my ribs!*" cried Ray.

"Oh, cripes!" said Roger. Throwing away the screwdriver, he thrust his hand into the control box and ripped out the entire panel.

"So much for keeping the circuits intact," said Trip dryly as the robot froze into inactivity.

Wendy came strolling into the cave just in time to see Trip and Roger finish cutting through Deathmonger's tentacle with a hacksaw. All three boys were streaked with sweat and dirt. Ray sagged between his friends like a survivor just pulled from a major accident.

Though Roger turned eagerly at the sound of Wendy's entrance, his shoulders drooped with despair when he saw that she was alone.

"Hey, don't be so glum," said the Wonderchild. "I found them, I just couldn't get at them. They've got the top brass in an uproar. Seems someone attacked Dr. Remov, and Hap and Rachel were the ones who found him." Wendy grimaced. "The doc was pretty bloodied up, from what I can make out. Anyway, Hap and Rachel dragged him to the infirmary, then roused Dr. Clark to take care of him. They've got half the island there now, trying to figure out what's going on. It's downright plasmagacious. The best thing is Brody. He's fit to be tied because he can't figure out how the missing robot connects with the attack on Remov—which makes sense, because it doesn't. But he's got it into his thick skull that it does, which is good for us, since the only thing harder than getting an idea into that mass of bone is getting an idea out of it. Hwa and McGrory are hovering like a pair of ducks, and Dr. Mercury—"

"Wait a minute!" yelled Roger. "You're going too fast. Let's get one thing clear. Are Hap and Rachel okay?"

"As near as I can tell. I picked up most of my information from the security band on the radio. I didn't want to get anywhere near that mess."

"And Dr. Remov?" asked Trip, who was quite fond of the tall, freckle-faced scientist.

"He's in pretty rough shape. They're not worried about him buying the farm. But he's not going to be doing any mountain climbing for a while, either."

"I didn't know Dr. Remov was a mountain climber," said Ray.

Wendy rolled her eyes.

"How did Hap and Rachel explain being out at this time of night?" asked Trip.

"They told Brody they were out on a date!" said Wendy, grinning wickedly. Turning to Roger, she added, "Boy, I'm glad I'm not going to be at your house tomorrow morning!"

The look on Anthony Phillips's face when he came to breakfast the next morning was enough to curdle the milk on his children's cereal.

"I received a very disturbing call from Dr. Hwa a little while ago," said Dr. Phillips as he took his seat at the table. *"Very* disturbing."

Roger frowned. When their father started repeating himself like that, it usually meant big trouble.

Rachel busied herself with her coffee.

"I don't know what the Swenson boy's parents think about this kind of thing," said Dr. Phillips, running his hand through his thinning auburn hair. "Personally, I find it deeply disturbing to be informed by my boss that my twelve-year-old daughter was out joyriding at two in the morning when I thought she was safely in bed!"

As a longtime student of cranky parent speeches, Roger had to give his father credit. This one was intense, yet too subdued to justify Rachel getting angry in response—always a good opening stance. The main problem was that it was also completely misinformed. Whether Dr. Phillips would have been any happier if he knew what was *really* going on was another question altogether. But Roger didn't like to see Rachel get in trouble for something that, as far as he knew, hadn't even crossed her mind.

His train of thought was interrupted when his father turned his attention from Rachel toward him. "I almost hate to ask this," said Dr. Phillips. "But knowing the way you two operate, I feel that I have to. Roger, did you know what was going on last night?"

Roger looked at his father with wide, innocent eyes. "Yes, sir, I did. As a matter of fact, it was my idea."

Dr. Phillips looked as if he was going to fall off his chair. "Would you care to explain that?" he asked, struggling to remain calm.

Rachel stared at her brother in fascination, wondering how he was going to wriggle out of this one.

At the moment Roger had no idea how he was going to get out of it. But his brain was operating at top speed. Clutching at the tablecloth, he stared his father straight in the eye. "Dad," he said seriously, "can I trust you?"

Dr. Phillips looked totally confused. "Haven't you got the question backward?"

Roger shook his head. "This is vitally important. It has to do with the robot."

Dr. Phillips blinked. *"What* robot?"

"Brody's robot! One of his security robots was captured last night. Didn't you know about that?"

"They don't keep me posted on security problems," said Dr. Phillips huffily.

"That's part of the problem! They don't keep anyone posted. That's why we were out last night. There's something weird going on around here, and we—"

"Now look," said Dr. Phillips, "I want you two to keep your lightly freckled noses out of things that are none of your business."

"Surviving here is everyone's business," said Roger softly. "If we had been keeping our noses clean last month, we wouldn't be here today—and neither would anyone else, since that wacko would have blown the whole island to kingdom come."

Dr. Phillips opened his mouth, then stopped. Roger was right: The entire population of Anza-bora Island owed their lives to the kids' "interference" in that security problem. He decided to change direction. "All right, do you know what happened to Brody's robot?"

"We're working on it."

Rachel gasped, then covered it by pretending she was choking. She couldn't believe her brother's audacity. His reply was perfectly honest, of course. But it was also open to two interpretations. In this case the truth—that they were actually working *on* the robot— was so outrageous that she was certain her father would opt to believe that they were working on *finding* it.

Dr. Phillips sighed. "I knew it wasn't going to be easy raising you two after we lost your mother, but honest to God, I never expected anything like this. Do me a favor, will you?"

"What is it, sir?" asked Roger, his voice filled with respect.

"Stay out of trouble."

"We'll try real hard."

In this, Roger spoke the absolute truth. He planned on working very, very hard to keep from getting caught.

12

Dr. Remov

DR. CELIA CLARK, THE NO-NONSENSE NEUROSURGEON who had switched to computers in the hope of finding a way to link brains to bytes, stood in front of the hall leading to Dr. Remov's room with her arms folded across her chest. Running the clinic was her share of the island's "housekeeping," and she ruled the place with an iron hand.

"I'm sorry, kids," she said firmly, "but Stanley does not need a mob descending on him right now. He has had all the excitement he can take for the time being. Two visitors is all I will allow, and that's final."

The gang moaned. Flushed by his earlier success in fast-talking his father, Roger stepped forward and offered a long and complicated explanation of why the rules should be bent on this occasion.

Pinching the bridge of her rather prominent nose, Dr. Clark listened carefully to Roger's reasoning.

Moving slowly, as if considering what he had said, she transferred her long, chestnut-colored braid from one shoulder to the other.

"You know, Roger, that almost made sense," she said at last. "Until I actually tried to sort out exactly what you said. At that point it took me only a moment to reach the inescapable conclusion that you had just spouted the biggest pile of horse puckey I have heard in a long time!"

"Defeat!" cried Roger. He slapped a hand to his forehead and collapsed into an institutional armchair.

Dr. Clark turned to the others. "All right, two of you are getting in. Who will it be?"

After a moment's conference it was agreed that as the "rescuers," Rachel and Hap should have the first chance to visit their friend.

"Don't take it too hard," whispered Rachel to her twin. "If you won them all, there'd be no living with you."

"Are you coming, Rachel?" asked Dr. Clark. "I don't have all morning!"

Rachel she had not had a chance to talk to Hap alone since the gang had convened that morning. So she took advantage of the walk down the hall to whisper, "What did *your* parents say about last night?"

Hap smiled. "My mom was pretty mad. But Dad told her to leave me alone. He said it just showed I was a chip off the old block. That didn't make her very happy, let me tell you! I'm afraid he'd be very disappointed if he knew why we were really out there. He's quite a romantic at heart."

Rachel made no response to this. But she did remind herself to avoid appearing too dreamy-eyed when she looked at her friend. *Settle down,* she told herself fiercely. *You've got more important things to think about right now.*

When Dr. Clark ushered them into the recuperation room they found Dr. Remov sitting up in bed, playing chess.

Rachel stifled a cry of shock. In the dark she hadn't been able to see how badly battered their friend really was. Though she had been horrified by all the blood, she had told herself that once it was washed off, he would look much better. She had been wrong. His heavily freckled face was so swollen and puffy it made her think of a toasted marshmallow; his cheeks were mottled with black and blue marks, a fierce shiner circled one eye, and a line of ugly stitches marched across his chin and down his neck.

"Ah, my rescuers!" cried Dr. Remov jovially. "Let me finish this game, and then we'll have a chat. I have some very important things to say to you." He looked up. "Thank you, Dr. Clark," he said in a voice that made it clear she was being dismissed.

Her face darkened a bit, but she stepped out of the room and closed the door. Remov smiled with one side of his mouth. "Stop trying not to look at me, Rachel. I know it's pretty awful. But as one computer scientist said to the other, I'm not ready to cash in my chips yet. Now be quiet for a minute while I figure out my next move."

He stared at the chessboard, his brow furrowed in concentration, then slid his queen three spaces to the right.

"Oh, sir, that *was* a wicked move," said his opponent, who happened to be a robot. Rachel and Hap watched in fascination as the silver-skinned automaton scratched its head, studied the board, then reached out and moved a bishop close to Dr. Remov's queen.

"Damn!" said the scientist. "Sometimes I think you machines have taken all the fun out of chess."

"What's his name?" asked Hap, nodding toward Dr. Remov's opponent.

"It!" said Dr. Remov crankily. "It, it, it! Don't try to make them any more human than they already are. Gender's the one thing they *don't* have—and never will, if we're lucky. Believe me, the last thing we need is a bunch of walking junkyards with hormone problems! Now let me finish this game."

Rachel turned her attention to Dr. Remov's opponent. Like a mermaid or centaur, the robot only looked human from the waist up. But instead of having a fish or horse for its lower half, it spread out to form a large, flat surface with a chessboard imprinted on the top. The whole contraption sat on a standard hospital table that extended across Dr. Remov's bed.

"The program itself is actually quite conventional," said Dr. Remov, as if he had read the questions in Rachel's mind. "The biggest challenge was building Egbert here so it could pick up and put down the pieces. And since the location of the chessboard is constant, even that wasn't much of a problem. The squares are always in exactly the same location relative to its arms."

"It's really wonderful, sir," said Hap.

"Thank you," said Dr. Remov. Then he picked up his queen and moved it to a new location.

"Wretched human!" cried Egbert. Stretching out a metallic arm, it swept the board, sending chess pieces flying in all directions.

Dr. Remov chuckled and rubbed his hands together. "Egbert is so much fun to beat!"

The robot closed its eyes and folded its arms over its chest.

"It'll stay that way till I push the reset button," said Dr. Remov. "Now, push the table aside for me and let's talk."

Hap did as the scientist asked. Then he and Rachel pulled their chairs close to the bed. Dr. Remov looked at them closely. He took a deep breath, then said, "We're in big trouble."

Rachel swallowed uneasily. The look in the scientist's eyes assured her that he was serious.

"What do you mean?" asked Hap.

"We have a new enemy on the island; a dangerous one. It was bad enough when we had to deal with G.H.O.S.T.—though you kids seem to be doing a good job of keeping *that* mess under control."

"Don't be too sure," said Rachel grimly.

Dr. Remov looked startled. "I beg your pardon?"

Hap looked around, then leaned forward and whispered, "It looks like Black Glove is back."

Speaking quickly the two kids told Dr. Remov about the glove Wendy's mother had found, and the threatening message that had arrived at Wendy's terminal the next morning.

Dr. Remov didn't seem surprised. "I was never certain the spy left to begin with," he said. "What concerns me now is how quickly he—or she—figured out that you had some new information. I suspect our E-Mail system is not really secure. Don't use it for anything you want to keep confidential."

Rachel shivered. But before she could respond, Dr. Remov went on. "All that is complicated by this fact: We now have another spy on the island. This one is a wild card. I don't know why he's here."

"You know who it is?" asked Hap.

Dr. Remov made an expression of disgust. "Yes. His name is Ramon Korbuscek. He's a former student of mine, from my days in the espionage business. A brilliant man, but totally devoid of morals, convictions, or beliefs."

"What does he look like?" asked Rachel.

"How would I know?"

Rachel blinked. "But you said—"

"I'm sorry, I guess that was a reasonable assumption on your part. But Ramon has almost certainly had his face altered at least a half dozen times since I last worked with him."

"Didn't you see him last night?" asked Hap.

Dr. Remov shook his head. "It was too dark, and the

fight was moving too fast." He snorted in disgust. "That whole thing was very stupid on my part. I'm not in bad shape, but I'm not honed to a fine edge like I used to be. And Ramon is in his prime. Of course, I didn't know it was Ramon when I jumped him."

"I'm confused," said Rachel. "If you didn't see him, and you wouldn't have known him if you had, how do you know it was him?"

"Style. Technique and tactics. Besides, he told me—just before he was about to knock me cold."

"No offense, sir," said Hap. "But why didn't he kill you when he had the chance?"

"Because he couldn't. That's how he told me who he was."

"Sheesh!" said Rachel. "Remember a minute ago I said I was confused? I take it back. *Now* I'm confused."

Dr. Remov chuckled. "When I was training Ramon, I had reason to hypnotize him on a number of occasions. We used it for concentration training, among other things. Well, you learn to protect yourself in that business. Part of *my* protection was to drill a posthypnotic command into the heads of my students, a key word that, uttered by me, would cause them to experience an attack of excruciating fear. That's what saved my skin last night."

He rubbed his freckled hands with satisfaction. "It was a strange fight from the beginning. My opponent's style was so familiar it was almost as if I were fighting myself. Suddenly it dawned on me who it might be. But it took me several seconds—some of the longest seconds of my life—to recall Ramon's key word. I whispered it just as he was about to knock me silly. When he leaped up and fled in terror, I knew that he was indeed Ramon."

Rachel's next question was interrupted by an exchange of angry voices in the hallway.

The first was unmistakably Dr. Clark's. "No, Armand, you will *not* go in there. I forbid it!"

"Forbid?" cried Dr. Mercury. "You *forbid* me? Celia, I am a natural force. You do not *forbid* me. Go out and yell at the tides if you wish. You will have better luck getting them to flow backward than you will in keeping me from seeing my friend."

"Armand!"

The door swung open and Dr. Mercury strolled in, looking none the worse for the wear. "What a wretched woman," he said to no one in particular. Then he looked at Dr. Remov. "Oh, Stanley!" he cried. "I adore your new look! The black and blue is so much more *colorful* than that plain old pallor and freckles you had been using for so long." He reached into his pocket and pulled out a pipe. "Do you mind?"

Dr. Remov shook his head. "You know I don't mind, Armand," he said wearily.

"Yes, I know. But since you're an invalid at the moment, I thought it would be nice to ask for a change."

Dr. Mercury extracted a small foil pouch from his pocket, then reached for the half-full glass of water that sat on the table next to the bed. Settling into a chair on the opposite side of the bed from the kids, he dumped powder from the pouch into the glass, stirred the water with his fingers, then dipped in his pipe.

"All ready," he said in satisfaction as he lifted the pipe to his lips. Concentrating for a moment, he blew an enormous bubble. Then he turned to Dr. Remov and said, "Now, what were we talking about? More of your crackpot theories, Stanley?"

Ignoring the sideswipe, Dr. Remov filled his friend in on their conversation. "What I can't understand," he concluded, "is how Ramon got on the island to begin with."

"Maybe he came in with that new batch of guards Brody ordered," suggested Hap.

Dr. Remov snapped his head around so fast Rachel was afraid he would injure himself. "What did you say?"

Hap repeated himself. "I've already spotted one I thought was suspicious," he added. "I didn't get a good look at him, though. All I know is that he has sandy hair."

"Well, that's two," said Dr. Remov.

"Two what?" asked Rachel.

"Clues! Ramon has always been right-handed—he can't change that. And he's dyed his hair sandy brown. So we're looking for a right-handed man with sandy-brown hair. Probably not enough to eliminate all the possibilities, but it's a start. If we could get our hands on the personnel records of those new men, it might help."

"Oh, that's no problem," said Rachel. "Wendy can just call them up on the computer."

A horrible silence descended on the room.

"What did you say?" asked Dr. Remov at last. He sounded as if he had a fishbone caught in his throat.

"Never mind. I know what you said. I just can't believe I heard it."

Ramon Korbuscek locked the door to the bathroom he shared with his roommate, then studied himself in the mirror. *Not too bad,* he thought, assessing the damage from last night's fight. *But certainly enough to attract attention.*

He took out a small makeup kit and began to cover the marks with a light powder. Makeup was one of the basic tools of his trade, and he worked smoothly and efficiently. As he did, his mind wandered to other things.

Primary among them was fear.

The fear he felt now was not caused by Dr. Remov's activation of the posthypnotic command—at least, not directly. That fear had faded soon after it hit.

What worried him now was the very fact of that fear. He had no memory of the secret word and how it affected him, so he didn't know *what* had caused his terrible panic last night, a fear unlike anything he had ever experienced before in his life.

A small voice in the back of his mind began to ask if perhaps his old teacher had some kind of control over him.

Korbuscek frowned. If that was so—and it seemed likely that it was—it would mean Remov knew he was on the island. And unless he, Korbuscek, took steps, sooner or later that could mean his undoing.

He sighed. Clearly Dr. Remov could not be allowed to live.

13

Rift in the Ranks

WENDY STARED INTO THE SKULL OF THE ROBOT THEY had captured and shook her head in dismay. "I wish Roger hadn't yanked that control panel. He made a total hash of the wiring. This thing looks like it's having the mental version of a bad hair day."

Hap Swenson shivered at the eerie sound of her voice echoing off the cavern walls. "Roger didn't have much choice," he pointed out, shifting the light he was holding to give her a better view of the wires. "The robot was squeezing Ray to death!"

"Ray's been getting a little porky lately anyway; he could stand a good squeeze or two." Wendy connected a pair of wires to see what would happen, then snapped, "Chips, Hap, will you hold that light steady?"

"Sorry. Let me see if I can find something to prop it up with."

He turned and began rummaging through the pile

of equipment they had stored in the cavern. "Oops! We'd better get these sound guns back to Dr. Mercury." He picked up one of the devices that had helped them bring down the robot, being careful not to pull the wires that connected them to the new attachments. "They worked pretty well, didn't they?"

"Not only did the guns work well," said Wendy in a rare moment of generosity. "Those extensions you added were perfect."

Of course, even with the two extra sound sources the gang had barely been able to subdue Deathmonger. Wendy's job now was to design a device that would give them total control over it—and all the others like it.

She pried away a panel she had found on the robot's chest. "Modular construction at last!" she cried. "Help me get these circuit boards out of here, Hap. Then we can take them back to headquarters to analyze how this thing works."

Hap didn't need any convincing. Unlike Trip, he had never been terribly fond of caves. They gave him the creeps.

Trip and Ray sat on either side of Dr. Remov, passing him hard-copy printouts of the personnel files for the eight new guards.

The files had been provided by Wendy, who had pulled them out of the computer at Dr. Remov's request.

Once he had gotten over his initial shock, the scien-

tist had been fascinated by the Wonderchild's ability
to crack the computer's security system. According to
Rachel, he had also been apologetic about what he
saw as his duty under the circumstances.

"I hate to mention this," he had said slowly. "But you
do know that I will have to report this sooner or later.
It's information that could be vital to the project."

Later, in private, Hap had told Ray that Rachel had
turned white when she heard Dr. Remov's words.

"Please don't do that," she had begged. "The others
will kill me if that happens!"

Dr. Remov had been silent for a moment, rubbing
his chin thoughtfully. "If Dr. Mercury is agreeable, I'll
offer you a compromise," he had said at last. "You
show me how the program works, and somehow Armand and I will get the information into the system
without telling anyone else where it came from. That
probably amounts to insubordination of some sort.
But one of the first things I learned in the spy business
was to protect my sources. If you kids are as smart as
you think you are, it won't take that long for you to
crack the system again anyway."

Under the circumstances, it seemed like a fair deal
to Ray.

"Here we go," said Dr. Remov, calling the Gamma
Ray's attention back to the matter at hand. "We have
two distinct traits for Korbuscek. With the help of the
files your friend provided, we now also know which
of the eight guards share those traits."

Trip and Ray leaned in to see what he had written.

Name:	Sandy-Haired	Right-Handed
Bigelow, Earl U.	X	X
Elliot, Martin B.		X
Freemont, U.P.R.		
Hopewell, Damon	X	X
Marston, Conrad T.	X	
Rosemunk, Brock A.	X	X
Sanders, Edward P.		X
Tidewater, Graham Q.	X	X

"As you can see, of the eight new guards six are right-handers and five have sandy-colored hair. But only four have both traits. So we've narrowed the field by half, bringing it down to Bigelow, Hopewell, Rosemunk, and Tidewater. If we can get one more attribute to put on the chart, we just might be able to nail down the new identity of Ramon Korbuscek, superspy."

Roger sat in front of the computer terminal in his room, rubbing his thumb and forefinger together so intensely he was in danger of burning the skin from the friction buildup. That was a sign of intense thinking with Roger, of course, and what he was thinking about was this: Dr. Remov was the only one of the adults who took their warnings about Black Glove seriously.

That *could* mean he was their best friend on the

island. Or it could mean that he himself was Black Glove. After all, what better way for the spy to keep track of what the gang was up to than to cultivate their friendship?

Roger shook his head. He was letting his fear get to him. Dr. Remov was far too tall to be Black Glove. They had to be rational about this.

Not that they didn't have good reason to be afraid. He thought back to the threatening message Wendy had received from Black Glove. How much access did their enemy have to their terminals anyway? Glancing at his own monitor, he had a momentary fantasy of Black Glove looking back at him. He shivered. What if the spy had managed to hook all the monitors into a system that would let him use them in reverse? What if he could see into any spot on the island that had a screen?

Roger snorted in disgust. He was being ridiculous.

He typed a command into his keyboard. If they were actually going to build this rocket, he needed to start learning the computer's design functions.

I wonder if Black Glove already knows we're going to build the rocket. I wonder if he even knows we're using it as bait? Roger rolled his eyes. *And I wonder why I think of Black Glove as being a male. No reason our spy couldn't be a woman. Between my sister and Wendy, I sure know how tough and smart females can be!*

A beep from the computer brought his attention

back to the information now appearing on his screen.

It quickly captured his interest. He had never built a rocket before. This should be fun!

"Hi, Twerpy," said Rachel glumly. She looked around. "Where's Dr. Weiskopf? He buzzed me in."

Not being programmed for speech, the robot didn't answer but simply continued to stand in a corner of the living room, singing to a plant.

Rachel was content to stand and listen. She loved the robot's music. After a moment Dr. Weiskopf appeared at the kitchen door, an apple enveloped in his huge hand. "Ah, Rachel! How are you this afternoon?"

She shrugged. "Not bad, I guess. I came to talk to you about the rocket."

"Good, good. It took me awhile to get used to the idea, but now I am most excited." He looked at her more intently. "What's the matter, Rachel? You look as if you just lost your best friend."

"Close enough."

Dr. Weiskopf studied her face for a moment. "Sit," he said, patting the couch. "Talk."

Rachel took a seat, but it was a minute before she could bring herself to say anything. When she did start, it seemed as if she couldn't stop. Checking herself as she spoke so she didn't make the same mistake again, she poured out the story of her indiscretion, her friends' dismay, and Wendy's anger.

Dr. Weiskopf nodded wisely. "I sometimes wonder if it was such a good idea for us to learn to talk. More friendships are lost over careless words than anything else. If there was only music, we might all be better off."

He reached into the pocket of his lab coat. "Here, have an apple. And just listen for a while.

He took out his pennywhistle and began to play for her. To Rachel's surprise, the song actually made her feet better. *Music has charms,* she thought.

After a few minutes Dr. Weiskopf gave her a nod that seemed to say: "Join me."

She took out her pennywhistle. Trying to follow his lead, she began to play, awkwardly at first, then with increasing fluency as she felt herself easing into the music.

Ramon Korbuscek opened his eyes and checked the position of the moon outside his window. It confirmed what his internal clock had told him: It was time to start the night's activities. Swinging his feet off his bed, he stood and stretched, his movements so smooth and silent his sleeping roommate didn't even stir.

Korbuscek glanced over at the snoring man. A pleasant-enough fellow, but in the way. It was time for him to go.

It was also time to find out something about these kids. Every time he turned around, he seemed to be crossing paths with them. The rumors he was hearing about their past escapades made him wonder if they might be more of a threat than he had anticipated.

Moving on the balls of his feet, he crossed to his roommate's dresser. It took only a moment to find what he needed.

Seconds later he had lowered himself out the window and was on his way.

After walking unnoticed through a network of streets, Korbuscek easily entered the Gammand residence. When he had finished there, he went on and prowled through the Swenson home.

When he reached his third target, however, Korbuscek hesitated before slipping the thin slice of metal he was using to open locks into the doorframe. From what he had been able to ascertain, this house was usually empty during the day. Perhaps it would be safer to come back then.

But he had already been in two homes tonight, and he was beginning to get a sense of the kind of things these kids were involved with. Not only was he feeling strong with success, his curiosity was operating at a high level.

Besides, there was one more thing he *had* to accomplish before he quit for the night.

So—inside it would be. Enjoying the familiar tingle of excitement, he slid the strip of metal along the edge of the door and popped the lock.

Drawing on years of practice, he opened the door without a sound. After he stepped into the house he stood for a long time, doing nothing but listening. The breathing told him that all three occupants of the house were asleep.

Heading away from the heavier breathing, he came to a door that was slightly open. The soft glow of a night-light showed through the crack. Giving the door a slight nudge with his fingers, he peered into the room.

Incredible! thought the spy. *I've seen bomb sites that had less rubble.*

He was looking, of course, into Wendy Wendell's bedroom.

14

The Intruder

RAMON KORBUSCEK TOUCHED A BUTTON AT THE SIDE of his electronic flashlight and played a low beam across the incredibly cluttered floor. There! A clear spot he could put one foot on! He stepped in and looked around. Another!

He grimaced. This was like finding stepping-stones to cross a stream.

The spy glanced over at the bed. The night-light showed a round, lightly freckled face. Pigtails stuck out at crazy angles from its sides.

Turning away from the bed, he raised his flashlight and played it along the opposite wall. It was lined with shelves, the shelves themselves cluttered with a strange mixture of electronic parts and childish toys, including a rather dilapidated-looking teddy bear.

Unaware of the photoreceptors Wendy had installed behind the bear's eyes, Korbuscek let his flashlight linger on the toy while he tried to make sense of all this.

To his alarm, the bear suddenly lurched its feet and growled, "Time to get up, Captain Wendy!"

Activated by its voice, Blondie the fashion doll stood up, too. "Morning already?" she cried. "That's gross!"

"Hey, Wendy!" bellowed a sweet-faced baby doll on the other side of the bear. "Move yer butt!"

Wendy snorted and flopped over in her bed.

Horrified, Korbuscek bolted for the door, tripped over an open toolbox, and crashed to the floor.

"Whazzat?" cried Wendy, sitting bolt upright. "Whozere?"

Korbuscek scrambled across the floor and out of the room, then down the hall and through the front door. On the bottom step of the porch he hesitated, then decided to take one last risk. Drawing a heavy object from the pack strapped on his back, he stooped and pressed it into the soft soil of the flower bed beside the step.

As he stood again he heard someone stumbling toward the door.

Korbuscek sprinted away from the house and faded into the darkness. He was long gone by the time Wendy's father, Dr. Werner Watson, opened the door and craned his head from side to side, seeking the intruder.

In her bedroom, Wendy flopped back and forth and a few more times, then began to snore again.

Trip Davis watched his father's long, paint-stained fingers deftly peel the shell from a hard-boiled egg.

"I'll tell you, Tripper," said Mr. Davis, trying to sound casual, "I'm not sure how much time you should be spending with those friends of yours."

Trip stared at his father in astonishment. "You've spent years telling me I should make more friends! Now that I've got some, you want me to give them up?"

"Oh, not necessarily give them up," said his mother, sliding her hand onto her husband's arm for support. "But maybe you should be more careful of what you let them talk you into. We just don't want you getting into a lot of trouble, sweetheart."

Trip took a deep breath to help keep him from saying something he shouldn't. He looked at his parents—his dark-haired, dreamy-eyed father and his ice-blond mother who could make a computer roll over and beg if she wanted to—and wondered if they really knew anything about him.

The unwelcome question that followed immediately on its heels was *How much do I know about them?* Trip tried to force the thought out of his mind. He didn't even want to consider the possibility that one of them might be the spy. But why were they so anxious for him to sever his ties with the gang? Did they know something he didn't? Was one of them plotting some trouble for his friends?

Trip felt his head begin to whirl. "I can't believe you people!" he shouted, pushing himself away from the table. "I just can't believe you!"

To his own surprise, he went stomping out of the house.

The scene at the Wendell-Watson breakfast table was not much calmer than that at the Davis house. However it was not Wendy who was at the center of this storm, but her nemesis, Sergeant Artemus P. Brody.

"What do you mean, you don't know?" cried Dr. Werner Watson, staring at Brody. "It's your business to know!"

Dr. Watson was still in his bathrobe. His jet-black hair, unruly at its best, looked like a battered bird's nest—its usual preshower condition. By contrast his wife, Dr. Wendy Wendell II, looked like a shampoo ad. Every strand of her shimmering golden hair was perfectly in place.

Both of Wendy's parents were staring scornfully at Sergeant Brody, who sat at their table with a steaming cup of coffee in his hands and a look of abject misery on his face.

"I'm sorry," repeated Brody. "I just don't know who could have broken into your house. And there's not a clue to be found."

"What about the footprint beside the front porch?" asked Wendy, always pleased with an opportunity to show Brody up.

"I must have overlooked that, missy," he said between his teeth. "Why don't you show it to me?"

"Gladly," said Wendy.

Dr. Remov looked up from his chessboard as Trip and Ray scurried into his room at the clinic.

"Have we got news for you!" said Ray, who looked as if he was about to burst.

"Another clue about Korbuscek," whispered Trip, closing the door so they wouldn't be overheard.

Speaking quickly, the boys detailed the story of the break-in at the Wendell house and Wendy's discovery of the footprint near her front door.

"Are you sure?" asked Dr. Remov when they had finished their recital.

"Absolutely," said Trip. "After Wendy showed Brody the footprint, he made a plaster cast of it. It's a regulation issue boot, the type used by the security guards. Size nine and a half."

"Get those folders," ordered Dr. Remov.

"They're right here, sir," said Ray. "I was expecting you would ask for them."

Adjusting his pillows behind his back, the freckle-spattered scientist pored through the files, checking a certain page in each one. "Get me the chart!" he said abruptly.

"You're holding it," replied Ray. "Bottom folder, last page."

Dr. Remov took it out and made a few rapid marks with a pencil. When he was finished, it looked like this:

Name:	Sandy-Haired	Right-Handed	Boot Size 9½
Bigelow, Earl U.	X	X	
Elliot, Martin B.		X	X
Freemont, U.P.R.			X
Hopewell, Damon	X	X	
Marston, Conrad T.	X		X
Rosemunk, Brock A.	X	X	
Sanders, Edward P.		X	X
Tidewater, Graham Q.	X	X	X

"Well," said Dr. Remov. "There you have it. Five men with size nine and a half boots. Five men with sandy-brown hair. And six right-handers. But only one man with all those traits combined."

"Then Graham Tidewater is our spy?" asked Ray eagerly.

Dr. Remov nodded.

Hap Swenson swallowed nervously. When the gang had asked him to enlist his father's help with the rocket project, he had agreed without a fuss. But now that it was time to ask, he was feeling a little nervous. His father was very practical. How he would react to such a "far out" idea was anybody's guess.

"Well," said Mr. Swenson, "are you going to stand there all day, or are you going to say what's on your mind?"

Hap swallowed again, then managed to squeeze out the question.

Henry Swenson looked at his son in astonishment. "Would I like to do *what?*"

"Help us build a rocket," repeated Hap.

Mr. Swenson put down his wrench and picked up a grease rag. He began wiping his hands. "Jeepers, Hap. You know I like doing hobby-type stuff with you. But you're old enough now I'd rather you only asked when you really needed me. With most of the men gone, I've got a lot to do these days, and—"

"I don't think you understand, Dad," said Hap. "I'm not talking about a model rocket. We've got something we want to put into orbit."

"I knew it!" cried his father, throwing down the rag. "I knew if you started hanging around with those eggheads from the mainland, you'd end up weird. I told your mother just the other day—"

"Dad, what's so weird? It's metal and motors, your favorite stuff. Just think of it as a very powerful car without the wheels."

Mr. Swenson stared at his son for a minute, then broke into a slow smile. "All right, I'll listen," he said. "That's all! Just listen. Now, what's this doohickey supposed to do?"

Sergeant Brody was still stinging from his early morning encounter with the Wendell family when he led a handpicked group of guards into the building where his new men were housed.

At a signal from Brody, the crew stopped outside the door to Ramon Korbuscek's room.

"This is it," said Corporal Peters. "We should find our intruder right in here."

"All right, men," said Brody. "Let's get him. But be careful. Dr. Remov warned me that this guy will probably have lethal weapons hidden on his body. Ready? And ... *now!*"

The lead guards kicked down the door and charged into the room, guns at the ready. The two men inside jumped to their feet, crying out in astonishment.

Without hesitation, two of the guards crossed to the right and grabbed Graham Q. Tidewater.

"Hey!" he cried. "What's going on?"

"You can drop the act, Mr. Korbuscek," snarled Brody. "I don't know how you managed to weasel yourself into this position, but we're wise to you now." He turned to the man who remained. "Sorry for the disturbance, airman. Look at it this way: You'll have a private room for a while. Just do me one favor in return and keep your mouth shut about this."

"Yes, sir!" said the man. He managed to snap off a stylish salute, despite his obvious astonishment at what had just happened.

"Okay, boys," said Brody. "Take him away."

The man remaining in the room waited until he was sure the guards and their prisoner had left the barracks. Once he was alone Brock A. Rosemunk—otherwise known as Ramon Korbuscek—permitted himself the luxury of a chuckle. The boot he had "borrowed" from his sandy-haired, right-handed roommate had done its work more efficiently than he anticipated. All he had really expected was to throw suspicion off his own size-ten track for a while.

Korbuscek's smile faded. There had to be several guards on the island who wore size nine and a half. The fact that someone—he doubted it was Brody himself; more likely it was Remov—had traced the boot he used last night to its true owner so quickly made him a little nervous.

On the other hand, now that they thought they had captured him, they would stop looking for him.

As long as he was careful, that should make his job much, much easier.

15

Computer Talk

ROGER HUMMED CONTENTEDLY AS HE ORDERED THE computer to enlarge the cargo section on his rocket design. The colorful image on the screen broke apart as the computer began to reformat the diagram. At the same time the program printed a list on the lower part of the screen of all the ways in which the change would affect the overall performance of the rocket.

"It'll never fly, Orville," said Paracelsus when the new diagram was complete.

Ignoring the automaton, Roger scanned the list and made notes of the major points. As he had expected, the correction created several new difficulties. He would have to come up with a way to solve them. But that was his job; the computer merely pointed out the problems.

Sometimes he wondered what people did before they had computer-aided design. CAD functions were so fast and efficient it was hard to imagine how many hours it would have taken just five years ago to do things he could now perform in a matter of minutes.

He thought of something his father liked to say: "The real question isn't how we got along without such things: It's what we're going to do now that we have them!"

Of course, that would be even more true if Project Alpha actually succeeded in turning ADAM into a computer that could truly think instead of merely executing programs.

But for now it was up to him, and this was just what he had been wanting to do—settle down and get to work. The gang's various adventures had been fun, but nothing beat the thrill of actually creating something. With Korbuscek in the brig and no new leads to follow on Black Glove, he could do just that.

Besides, with luck this rocket would draw their enemy out of hiding.

While Roger applied himself to designing Euterpe's rocket, the two female members of the A.I. Gang were hard at work in the neighboring room.

Wendy was running tests on the control modules she had removed from the security robot. They weren't that complicated once she had determined the theory behind them. But the work was time-consuming. She glanced over at Rachel, who was humming quietly to herself as she passed page after page of information through the optical scanner they had attached to the Sherlock terminal.

Wendy scowled and jabbed angrily at the circuit

board with her micropliers. She wanted to say something to Rachel, but she didn't know how. What really bugged her was that she had gone from being the wounded party to being the villain.

It had happened when Rachel had come to her with an apology the day after she told Dr. Remov about Wendy's password program. It had been a first-class apology: Rachel had admitted it was all her fault, talked about how awful she felt, and asked to be excused for the error.

Unfortunately, instead of accepting the apology, Wendy had been scathingly sarcastic and said some things—well, several things—that she now wished she had kept to herself.

Since then, Rachel hadn't spoken a word to her unless absolutely necessary.

The solution, Wendy knew, was simple. It was her turn to apologize. But it made her angry to have to come up with an apology when the whole mess had all been Rachel's fault to begin with.

Besides, she didn't do apologies.

"Hi, guys!" said Ray, bounding through the door with his basketball firmly in his grip. "How's it going?"

The most articulate responses came from Norman the Doorman, who said, "Greetings and welcome!" and Rin Tin Stainless Steel, who barked, "Hi, handsome!" The girls looked up and grunted their greetings, but neither actually spoke.

"Almost ready to rearrange that robot's brain?" asked Ray, looking over Wendy's shoulder at the circuit board.

"Bug off!" she snapped.

"Right," said Ray. "I figured you'd say that."

Nice work, Wendy, thought the Wonderchild. *Keep it up and maybe they'll find a nice hole for you to work in so you don't keep offending civilized people.*

Ray dribbled his ball across the room to where Rachel was working. "How's it going, partner?" he asked, hoping for a friendlier response than he had gotten from Wendy.

"Jmphgurg," replied Rachel, trying to talk around the pencil she had clenched between her teeth.

Ray accurately translated this to mean, "Just a minute—" He put down his basketball and sat on it. His use of the word *partner* had been deliberate, since he was also assigned to the scanner project.

He had been assigned to it primarily because of his glitch-spotting abilities. When Rachel was trying to get the computer to actually understand what she had given it to read, it was usually Ray who could spot the break in communications between human and machine. He didn't know how he did it; it was just an ability he had.

Rachel finished what she was doing and looked up, then down to where Ray sat. "Hi."

"Feeling nonverbal?"

She shrugged. "Actually, I feel like I've got words coming out my ears. I've fed a small library into this thing. But I still can't figure out what ends up in the comprehensive memory and what remains in isolated cells."

"What's comprehensive memory?" asked Hap, who

had come in along with Trip just in time to hear the end of Rachel's comment.

Wendy looked up from the control panel with a witty remark about ignorant grease monkeys on the tip of her tongue. To her enormous relief, she managed to squelch it before the words escaped and did her more damage.

"It's the computer's general working memory," said Rachel. "The stuff it can draw on without being instructed to look for it specifically. The comprehensive memory also holds the things it can do without a lot of special instructions: number crunching, word processing, tasks like that. The more comprehensive memory a computer has, the 'smarter' it is."

"And isolated cells?"

Rachel frowned. "Well, having an isolated cell is a little like memorizing a formula from a physics book without understanding what to do with it. The information is there, but it doesn't do you much good. Right now this computer has a lot of specific knowledge without knowing what to do with it." She paused and frowned. "Was that clear?"

Hap grinned. "Like mud."

"Let me see if I can think of an example." She paused again and rolled her eyes sideways, as if she was actually looking into her brain for the answer. "Let's try this one. The computer 'knows' plants can't grow without water."

"How do you know it knows that?" asked Wendy, drawn into the conversation in spite of herself.

"I don't, I'm just trying to set up an example. Now, let's say it also knows that there's no water in the Sahara. But it holds those facts in isolation. So if I ask if plants can grow in the Sahara, unless I tell it how to get the answer, it doesn't know. That's isolated cells.

"Now, the material in the comprehensive memory has been integrated. That means that in the structure of the computer's functions, it can be applied in many different ways, to many different problems. I hate to use this word, but you can almost think of it as material the computer *understands.*

"The problem I'm having now is that when I feed material through the scanner, I don't know what it's going to integrate and what information will end up as useless facts."

"I thought that was the whole point of attaching the scanner," said Hap. "To build up its supply of facts."

"Useful facts," said Rachel. "Although the 'useless' ones aren't entirely wasted. They'll be there when the time comes."

"What time?" asked Roger, walking through the door. "Lunchtime, I hope."

"No, pea brain. The time of critical mass when all this comes together and brings the computer to the next step of awareness. Right now my big job is moving stuff from the isolated cells to the comprehensive memory. But the more stuff you get in there, the easier it gets."

"Which means the smarter it gets, the faster it can get smart," said Roger. "Until finally it reaches the Breakthrough Point, and then Bingo! It puts *everything* together. All that knowledge, completely integrated. It will be *awesome*. Now can we eat? I'm hungry!"

"How are the rocket plans coming?" asked Hap.

"No problemo. We start construction tomorrow!"

A rocket.

Black Glove stared at the wall of the secret room without really seeing it. Those crazy kids were actually building a rocket for that crackpot Weiskopf and his singing robot.

The funniest part was, it would probably work. They were just bright enough to pull it off—especially with the help they could get from some of the more soft-hearted scientists.

Hands pressed together, Black Glove drummed one set of leather-covered fingertips against the other. After a time a slow smile creased the spy's face. Interesting possibilities were beginning to present themselves.

This rocket could be the key to solving my communications problem. Which means there doesn't have to be any "probably" when it comes to the success of the thing. I'll just make sure they get all the help they need!

Black Glove chuckled. *Yes, that's it. We'll all help each other! I'll do whatever I can to make sure the rocket gets built successfully. In return, those brats will give me a perfect way to start getting information off the island again!*

"That's it!" said Wendy. "I think it's going to work!"

"Shall we give it a trial run?" asked Hap, snapping the back onto the black plastic case he had just finished rewiring.

"Why Dr. Swenson—I thought you'd never ask! Let's drive over to the cavern and see if we can't make Deathmonger sit up and whistle Dixie for us."

Hap insisted on driving, much to the Wonderchild's annoyance.

"You attract too much attention," he explained. "Partly because you drive so fast—partly because people can barely see your head above the wheel and they think the dune buggy is driving itself!"

It was only the fact that they were driving along a narrow road that edged a steep drop to the ocean when he said this that saved Hap from the Wonderchild's wrath.

Deathmonger was waiting in the cavern, right where they had left it.

"Hi, gorgeous," said the Wonderchild, patting the fanged monstrosity. "Ready to strut your stuff for your new boss?"

"He's not talking," said Hap. "Must be in a bad mood."

"We'll see about that!" Wendy pressed a button on the remote control. Immediately Deathmonger's eyes began to flash. A low grumbling sound issued from its center.

"Contact!" crowed Wendy.

She pushed another button, and the robot began to roll in their direction.

"Not so close!" cried Hap. "That thing still makes me nervous."

"Do you take back that crack about my driving?" asked Wendy.

"I take it back, I take it back!" said Hap. "Now get that thing away from me."

Wendy punched another button and the robot turned right. "This is all pretty elementary," she said as she directed the robot through a series of figure eights. "But I think we've got the problem licked. Now we need a control box for each of us, and the code numbers for the other robots. Of course, if my password program was still working, I could just call those up on the computer."

"Give it a rest, will you?" said Hap. "We're all waiting for you and Rachel to patch things up so we can get back to normal."

Wendy acted as if she hadn't heard him. "Come here," she said. "I want you to help me with a little surprise I've got in mind. Then we can take Deathmonger here home."

"That's going to be a relief," said Hap. "Brody's been like a mad dog since the thing disappeared. I can't say as I blame him. He's got to know we have it. He just can't figure out what we did with it."

"Probably thinks we took it out to sea and sank it," said Wendy. "One of the many things that bothers me about that clown is he's the only person I know who thinks I get away with more than I actually do."

"As opposed to your parents," said Hap, "who would die if they knew even half of it."

"I can't believe it," said Dr. Weiskopf, looking at the array of parts that stretched across the floor of the abandoned hangar. "I never thought you would get this far."

"We're determined little devils," said Roger, flipping down his safety visor so he could resume welding. "I think we'll be ready to launch before the month is over."

"I'm delighted!" said Dr. Weiskopf. "Of course, that means I have a lot to do myself. I need to get Euterpe into tiptop shape for her journey. And the sensors still need some work. Plus I've got to check the gravity compensators . . ."

He wandered away, ticking off the tasks on his sausagelike fingers. Rachel smiled as she watched him leave. "What a sweet little man," she said fondly.

Mr. Swenson gave her a bemused look. "Do you know what his nickname used to be?"

The twins shook their heads.

"I do," said Trip, who was measuring a sheet of metal for a fin. "He was called 'The Sword of the Desert.' "

"The Sword of the Desert?" echoed Rachel. "Why, for heaven's sake?"

"He was one of the most respected soldiers in the Middle Eastern wars of a few decades back," said Mr. Swenson. "He had a reputation for killing swiftly, and without mercy."

"Dr. Weiskopf?" asked Roger incredulously.

"Yes. He . . . uh-oh. Looks like trouble."

Roger turned to follow Mr. Swenson's gaze.

Dr. Hwa had just walked through the door of the hangar, Bridget McGrory striding along beside him.

"Well," said Dr. Hwa, surveying the accumulation of parts. "This is quite a project you youngsters have developed. I'm most impressed."

"Please don't make us stop," pleaded Rachel. "We're not hurting anything, and it means so much to Dr. Weiskopf. It really won't be any problem. And—"

"My dear girl, you misunderstand me," said Dr. Hwa, holding up his right hand. The large ruby ring he always wore glittered as it caught a stray beam of light reflecting off the rocket. "I don't want you to stop work. I will say I am quite offended that no one saw fit to tell me about this little project. But I'm here to give it my blessing."

Rachel had been about to launch into another defense of the project. Her jaw hung open as she tried to assimilate the meaning of Dr. Hwa's words.

"Actually," he continued, "I've been concerned about staff morale for some time. Between the isolation and the security problems, group spirit is not what it should be. A project like this could provide some useful diversion."

"Makes sense to me," said Roger.

"I think you'll be interested in this," said Dr. Hwa, extending a carefully folded sheet of paper in Roger's direction.

16

Twerps in Space

ROGER OPENED THE PAPER. INSIDE, WRITTEN IN A tight, tidy hand, was a seemingly meaningless string of numbers and letters.

Dr. Hwa chuckled at the puzzled look on Roger's face. "It's a security code for the computer. One of many," he added pointedly. "Don't expect it to give you unlimited access to our classified files!"

Rachel blushed, wondering if despite Dr. Remov's assurances, information about Wendy's password program had somehow reached Dr. Hwa.

"What you *can* access with this," continued Dr. Hwa, "are the original plans for Air Base Anza-bora, and an inventory of materials left behind by the Air Force. That should prove useful to you. Among other things, this will give you the locations of some missile silos. You may find using one of them more efficient than trying to build a launchpad from scratch."

"I . . . I don't know what to say," stammered Roger.

"Which is almost unheard of for him," said Rachel. "But if he was thinking straight, he might start with 'thank you.' We really are very grateful, Dr. Hwa."

The little scientist waved his hand in a gesture of dismissal. "I only hope you will open this to the other researchers so that they can participate as well. As I said, I think it will be good for morale. You see, Rachel, at heart I am a pragmatist. My offer may *seem* generous, but it is also good for me. The best arrangements always work that way." He smiled, then added, "I had one more reason, quite compelling, to offer my assistance."

"What was that?" asked Roger.

"Safety. I was worried that you might blow yourselves to kingdom come. Pragmatically speaking, that would be very bad for the project. Besides, I have grown quite fond of you, and so would prefer to keep that from happening. My assumption is that the more expertise you have to draw on, the less likely you are to come to a sad, if spectacular, end."

He turned to Mr. Swenson. "Please be sure to let me know if I can help in any way."

Then he pivoted on his heel and walked away.

"I can't believe it!" said Roger. "I was sure he was going to tell us to stop."

"That shows what you know," said Bridget McGrory, who had lingered behind. "That man is the salt of the earth. And it's about time you kids learned it!"

She started to walk away, too, but turned back. In

her lilting Irish brogue she said, "By the way, if any of you happen to know who left a robot wrapped in red ribbon on Sergeant Brody's doorstep last week, you can tell them from me that it was a job well done. I have it on good authority that when he opened the door and the robot started to sing 'Happy Birthday,' Brody darn near broke down and cried."

She gave them a wink, then scurried to catch up with her boss.

"One of Anza-bora's many mysteries," said Rachel. "I can never figure out if that woman loves us or hates us."

"I think it's both," said Roger. "But when it comes to Brody, there's no question. She has no positive feelings at all."

While Dr. Hwa and his secretary were examining the gang's progress on the rocket, Ramon Korbuscek was examining Sergeant Brody's mail. He sat with his feet on the security chief's desk, leafing through the letters and memos. He had started going through Brody's mail about a month earlier, and already the habit had proved quite useful. For example, he had recently intercepted a top-secret letter suggesting that Brody do some checking in regard to a guard named Brock A. Rosemunk.

Naturally, he had destroyed *that* little bombshell before it got anywhere near Brody's eyes.

He had also known before anyone else on the base that poor Graham Tidewater had been transferred back to the mainland to face a court martial for treason.

The removal of Tidewater created an excellent operating situation for Korbuscek, since it tended to make everyone believe they had gotten rid of the spy. This greatly enhanced his freedom of movement.

He had already used that freedom to good advantage by making several swings through Weiskopf's quarters. He now had a complete photo-record of the documentation for Euterpe—material that should fetch a high additional price from his current employers when he turned it over to them.

Unfortunately, what he had not been able to do was tamper with the robot itself. And that was vital— especially since he had found out they were actually planning to send the damn thing into space. But Weiskopf took it into his room to sing him to sleep every night.

That alone wouldn't have stopped Korbuscek, of course. But according to some of the notes he had photographed, Euterpe was equipped with an alarm system that would just about raise the dead if anyone tried to tamper with it.

So he had been avoiding that task. But it had to be done, and soon, because the launch date was fast approaching.

Korbuscek swung his feet off Brody's desk, stood, and chuckled. Watching those kids in action had been one of the best things about this assignment. They were a riot.

He almost hoped he wouldn't be forced to hurt them before this was over.

Dr. Hwa's invitation for his staff to participate in "Operation Euterpe" had had exactly the effect he predicted. The nimble minds of the small scientific community had leaped at the chance for a diversion.

Between the name of the robot and the fact that the whole project had been generated by the kids, it hadn't taken long before someone suggested calling the project "Twerps in Space."

When Trip's father designed a logo featuring a robot, a rocket, and that slogan, the name was official.

At first Roger worried that the project would be taken out of their hands. But the adult scientists, always protective of their own turf, seemed to respect the fact that the gang had staked out this territory first. Their behavior was like that of the ideal houseguest: They pitched in to help, but never demanded that things be done their way.

And when Dr. Hwa hired Ray's mother to make a set of coveralls for everyone in the gang, each specially embroidered with the "Twerps in Space" logo, they felt it was definitely their project.

In fact, there were only two bleak spots for the gang in all this time.

First was the continuing tension between Rachel and Wendy. They were cordial to each other now; certainly there was nothing that would be noticeable to an outsider. But within the group there was a sense that things were not as tight as they had once been. Something precious had been lost, and no one was certain how to get it back.

Second was the question of Black Glove—a question that became more pressing when they entered the headquarters one morning to find a message on Sherlock's main screen:

To: The A.I. Gang
From: A Friend
Re: Our Mutual Enemy

Warning! The person you call Black Glove has plans to subvert the launch. This agent is desperate, and may do anything at this point.

Proceed with extreme caution. Guard against deceit. Do not let yourself be fooled by smiling faces.

I have watched you for some time now. You are doing good work. Unfortunately, I cannot reveal myself at this point. But you should know that you do have a friend who understands your problems.

"Plasmagunderundum!" cried Wendy. "What kind of message is that?"

"I think *cryptic* is the word," said Rachel coolly.

"Maybe it's really from Black Glove himself," said Ray. "Or herself. Whatever. I bet it's just to scare us off."

"Could be," said Trip. "But by now he or she knows enough about us to know we don't scare easily."

"Well, I've had more useful 'friends,' " said Roger. "I can think of lots of things we could use more than a warning."

"I'm not so sure about that," said Hap. "Maybe we've been getting a little careless in the last few weeks. It's been so long since we saw any sign of Black Glove, we stopped worrying about him that much. A kick in the pants might be just what we needed at this point."

"Hap could be right," said Rachel. "And the game's not over until the last play; our unknown friend might have something more substantial to offer before everything is finished. But I sure hate to think of anyone trying to mess up the launch. Everyone has worked so hard on it."

"I doubt Black Glove will try to mess it up," said Trip. "That rocket isn't going to hurt her any. And if she still hasn't come up with any other way to get information off the base, it could be the answer to her problems. When our mysterious friend talks about Black Glove trying to subvert the launch, I bet she means the spy is going to try to slip some sort of transmission device on board. But that was just what we were counting on—that the rocket would be a trap to catch the spy in action."

"I just hope he doesn't catch us first," muttered Hap.

*   *   *

Two months later, on a sunny afternoon in mid-October, Rachel Phillips stood at the bottom of a concrete tunnel, leaning against one of the fins of Euterpe's rocket.

Dr. Hwa had been right. Being able to use one of the existing missile shafts had saved them an enormous amount of work. It had been easy to open, far easier than building a scaffold outside would have been. To the gang's delight, it had also turned out to be in perfect working condition.

"Well, why not?" Hap had wanted to know when the others expressed their surprise at this. "If you build something right the first time, it ought to keep working forever—or at least until the parts wear out. And nothing has happened to this to wear it out."

"Boy, do you live in a dreamworld," snorted Roger. "Long-term use is not the American way these days."

Rachel had tuned out the discussion that followed. But now she found herself wondering how long Twerpy would last out in space. She was going to miss the silly-looking robot. Its music had become an important part of her life.

Her reverie was broken by the voice of Dr. Ling, who was helping with the countdown checkoff. "Let's hurry," said the beautiful scientist. "This place gives me the creeps."

She was standing next to Rachel, dressed in a regulation lab coat and a white baseball cap that made her raven hair appear even darker and glossier than usual.

In her hand she had an electronic clipboard with a countdown checklist.

"What is it that bothers you about this place?" asked Roger, who was standing on the other side of Dr. Ling.

Rachel was pleased to hear a note of genuine curiosity in his voice. It drove her crazy when she thought her twin was toadying up to the lovely scientist.

"Consider what it was built for," said Dr. Ling. "It used to house an atomic missile. Remember, this was a first-alert station for the next war." She shuddered. "Besides, this cramped space makes me claustrophobic."

Rachel could understand that. Though nearly forty feet deep, the concrete shaft was only ten feet square. Its floor and walls were smooth and bare except for three things: the trapdoor in the floor through which they had entered; a clock to tell workers how much time they had before blastoff; and a ladder—no more than oversize metal staples, really—that led up the wall to the catwalk above.

Rachel looked around the floor. It was smaller than her bedroom's. She shivered at the thought of being caught here when the rocket blasted off. She had seen films of that first incredible surge of flame and the agonizing moments when the rocket was fighting free of Earth's gravity. At that moment this concrete box would be wall to wall searing flames. Would even your bones would be left if you were trapped in such an inferno?

Oh, stop it, she chided herself. *You've got work to do.*

Leonard Weiskopf stood at the top of the missile shaft, looking down. He still couldn't believe his robot was finally going to make it into space—much less that they had built the beautiful silver needle that would carry it there right here on Anza-bora Island.

He watched the group at the bottom of the shaft scurrying about, making last-minute checks. Then he turned his attention to Euterpe. "Are you ready?" he asked, wiping the robot's chest panel with a clean handkerchief. "This is what you were made for, you know."

Euterpe trilled a little tune, her light grid flashing rhythmically. She was operating the "music of the spheres" program.

Dr. Weiskopf lifted his hand to the side of the Beethovenly face and flipped a switch.

Then he took out his pennywhistle and began to play.

A moment later Euterpe answered him. Soon they were jamming, the unearthly music echoing strangely from the walls of the missile silo.

When the session was over, Dr. Weiskopf patted the robot fondly. "I'm going to miss you, Euterpe," he whispered. He pointed upward. "Do a good job out there."

Then he turned and walked away.

An hour later the final checks had been made.

When everyone had called in his final reports, the launch clock was set in motion.

Even though the launch clock was ticking, it was nearly eight o'clock that evening before the gang and the scientists working with them finished attending to the last-minute details.

When they polished off the last of their checklists Dr. Fontana said, "Well, that's it. We might as well call Brody."

A few minutes later the burly chief of the air patrol appeared in the control tower where the launch group had been working and shouted, "Everybody out! I'm sealing it up!"

Kids and scientists filed out of the room together, deeply engaged in an assortment of conversations and arguments about the upcoming launch. Brody stuck his head through the door and did a quick check to make sure everyone was out, then locked the room with his master key.

Wendy Wendell waited another half hour before she crept from behind the control panel where she had been hiding.

17

The Missile Silo

WENDY'S SELECTION AS "INSIDE MAN" AT THE SITE WAS prompted by two facts: First, her size made it easier for her to hide than anyone else in the gang except Ray. Second, unlike Ray, her parents kept a loose rein on her. A few mumbled comments about spending the night with Rachel so they could go to the launch together in the morning was all it had taken to cover her whereabouts.

Despite the fact that she and Rachel were still barely speaking to each other, what she had said was technically true. What she hadn't specified was that she, Rachel, and the rest of the gang would be spending the night *at* the launch site, in the hope of catching Black Glove in action.

Wandering to the front of the control tower, she gazed down on the net of humans and robots crisscrossing the airfield and its surrounding areas. *This is weird,* she thought. *Except for Dr. Remov, none of the adults will even admit Black Glove exists. Yet the brass on this supposedly private island is acting like there's a real risk of someone tampering with the launch. I guess the Korbuscek episode scared them more than they want to admit.* She smiled. *At least we don't have to worry about* him *tonight.*

A pair of searchlights crossed in front of the control-tower windows, looking like giant light sabers ready to do battle. Euterpe's music, piped in from a direct connection to the robot, played softly in the background.

Wendy pushed back her work hat and dug through the pockets of her "Twerps in Space" coveralls. After a little searching she retrieved a candy bar and a small pocket watch.

She sighed. Another three hours until Rachel, Roger, and Hap were scheduled to arrive. There had been a bit of a security crackdown on the domestic side of the island, too, and Trip and Ray would be even later, depending on what time their parents fell asleep. Fortunately, with the launch scheduled for seven A.M. sharp, even the strictest of the parents had agreed the kids needed to be out before dawn to be on hand for the final preparations. They were expecting their kids to leave early—just not as early as the kids themselves had in mind.

Actually, the excuse of making last-minute checks was a little lame. The launch pattern was already locked into the computer, and the takeoff could only be altered under extraordinary circumstances, and then only with extreme difficulty.

Wendy yawned. She had better find something to keep herself busy if she was going to be awake when it was time to let the others in. She patted her pocket. The control device for Brody's robots was right where she had put it.

She wandered around the control room, trying out the various chairs. She felt a little silly—*Like Goldilocks and the Three Astronauts,* she thought—but getting access to this place had been a real thrill. It made everything seem so real, so professional.

She glanced at the launch clock and frowned. Still two hours before the others would arrive! Leaning her face against the window, she began to count the robots scurrying around below.

Two minutes later her eyes closed and she began to snore.

Ramon Korbuscek slipped from his guard post and headed for the missile silo. Since he was a part of security, it was not that hard for him to breach it. All he had to do was alter his assigned patrol, take care of his "personal business," and then be back in time for his regular check-in. As long as he wasn't late, no one would suspect a thing.

Actually, Korbuscek would rather have performed this task on any other night. But Weiskopf's robot had not been loaded into the rocket until this afternoon, and he had finally decided that if he tampered with it any earlier his work might have been discovered—and removed—before the launch. By waiting until now, he could be fairly certain what he did would remain untouched.

Slipping through the shadows, he made his way to the maze of tunnels that crisscrossed the area under the airfield. It had taken him several nights of exploration to learn them well enough to move freely and without hesitation. Now he could find his way through them blindfolded.

Following a tunnel he had located three days earlier, he quickly came to the door that opened onto the upper level of the missile silo.

A narrow catwalk led over the forty-foot chasm of the silo to the door of the rocket. When Korbuscek found himself dancing along it like a tightrope walker, he realized how bored he had become. It felt wonderful to be in action again.

Pressing a sequence of panels, he opened the door of the rocket and stepped inside. Euterpe stood in the middle of the chamber. The lights on the robot's chest were flashing as it computed the music of the spheres.

Korbuscek made a snort of disgust. *That is the dumbest-looking robot I have ever seen.*

Foolish as the thing looked, the music it was creating was altogether remarkable. To Korbuscek's astonishment, it made the small hairs on the back of his neck rise. He shivered. Nothing had affected him like that in a long time.

But he wasn't being paid to judge the quality of the robot's music. His job was to alter its capabilities.

Squatting in front of Euterpe, he pulled a complex device from his backpack and prepared to install it.

The workspace was cramped, but he had plenty of time. Holding a pair of micropliers, he studied the front of the robot. Getting into something like this was a little like performing an operation. Recalling the diagrams he had photographed, he reached out and touched what he thought was the right spot to begin.

Immediately Euterpe began to shriek like an opera singer whose shower has just run out of hot water.

Korbuscek cried out in pain and clamped his hands over his ears. Pushing himself against the wall of the rocket, he tried desperately to recall where the diagrams had indicated the key to turn off the alarm. But the shrieking was making it impossible to think. He clamped his eyes shut and used a deep-breathing technique to relax himself enough to concentrate.

Right! He had it.

He took his hands from his ears. The shrill alarm, amplified terribly by the small chamber, caused tears to form in his eyes. Wondering if his hearing would be permanently damaged, he groped desperately over the robot's chest panel until he found the switch to turn off the alarm.

Immediately Euterpe stopped shrieking and began to sing again.

Sweat pouring down his face, Korbuscek collapsed against the robot and tried to recover his equilibrium.

*　　*　　*

The Phillips twins and Hap Swenson crouched at the edge of the airfield, just outside the range of the guards and the robots. The dark blue of their coveralls helped them blend into the surrounding darkness.

Gaining entrance to the restricted area would not be as simple for them as it had been for Korbuscek. Even as that spy was working his way toward the missile silo, the trio was waiting impatiently for Wendy to alter the pattern of the robot patrol so they could sneak past it.

Roger checked his watch as two of the fierce-looking things crossed in front of them for the fifth time.

"What's going on?" he muttered. "Why doesn't she redirect them?"

"I don't know," said Hap. "Do you suppose something could have happened to her?"

"I doubt it," said Rachel. "I learned a long time ago not to worry about Wendy. The question is, what do we do now? We've *got* to get in there."

"Maybe we should tackle the robots ourselves," said Hap. He didn't sound happy about the idea. "I wish Trip and Ray were here," he added.

Aside from Wendy, who had designed the robot control mechanism, Trip and Ray were the only ones who could be considered really expert with the device—largely because they had gotten so much practice with it on their scrounging missions.

Roger pulled one of the black boxes out of his pocket and looked at it uncertainly. "I don't know. It's a bit of a chance."

"We've *got* to get in there," repeated Rachel. "If we don't, Black Glove may pull whatever he's got in mind before we can get in position, and we'll have lost our chance to get a photo!"

As she spoke, she touched the miniature camera, no bigger than a stick of gum, that hung around her neck.

"All right, we'll give it a try," said Roger. He studied the control device for a minute, then whispered, "Be ready to move. I'll try to stop them the next time they cross by."

The three youngsters tensed themselves for action. Suddenly the robots rolled into view, sooner than they had expected.

"Now!" said Roger, pushing a button.

Anticipating that the robots would stop, he stepped forward.

He had anticipated wrong. The mechanical sentinels wheeled and headed straight for him, their red eyes flashing. Roger jabbed desperately at the controls. Nothing happened.

"Run!" cried Rachel.

It was too late. Roger felt the blood drain from his face as the lead robot reached out and snatched him into the air.

18

Down for the Countdown

THE SOUND SYSTEM CARRYING EUTERPE'S MUSIC INTO the control tower had helped lull Wendy into a deep sleep. Now that same sound system carried the shrieking of the robot's alarm, which would have roused any normal human to instant wakefulness, and did indeed actually begin to penetrate the Wonderchild's slumber.

"Whazzat?" she muttered, lifting her head. "Whozere?"

The alarm sounded for another thirty seconds, then abruptly fell silent.

Someone's going to pay for this, thought Wendy as she pushed herself away from the window. She wiped the drool from her squashed cheek, a dazed expression on her face. Where was she, anyway?

Suddenly everything came back to her. The launch! The robots! She glanced up at the clock. She was late! The others would be waiting for her.

She barreled out of the control room and headed down the stairs. Seconds later she emerged from one of the small buildings at the edge of the airfield—just in time to spot a robot snatch Roger into the air.

This, she thought dismally, *is not gonna enhance my reputation.*

Moving into high speed, she raced across the blacktop, ducking a searchlight that swept across her path. As she ran, she searched her pockets for the control box.

It was missing! It must have fallen out while she was asleep!

"Take this one!" cried Hap, tossing his own control to her as she came running up.

She caught it just as the second robot was about to grab Rachel. "Take that!" she cried, jabbing one of the buttons. "And that!"

The robots froze in position.

"Wendy," said Roger quietly. "How very nice of you to come. Do you suppose you could get me down from here?"

"Sure thing, Chief," said the Wonderchild, snapping him a salute.

She twisted a dial and pushed a button.

The robot set Roger gently onto the ground.

"Where have you been?" asked Rachel angrily.

"No time for that now," said Roger, interrupting

before tempers could really flare. "Let's get to our stations!"

Rachel nodded. Since she had stored the plans for the airfield and its tunnels in her highly trained memory, the next move was up to her.

Success is almost at hand, thought Black Glove, caressing the device that would reestablish contact with G.H.O.S.T. *All I have to do is get this transmitter into the rocket and I have a first-class communications satellite that will enable me to send the Executive Council everything we do here.*

A grim smile lit the spy's face. Waiting until the last moment had been difficult, but it was the only way to avoid detection. And that was important, for this time there could be no mistakes. Nor could there by any interference. The moment for gentle persuasion was past. Those foolish brats had been warned. If they tried anything tonight, their fate would be on their own heads.

Stepping out of the secret room beneath the computer center, Black Glove chuckled at the thought, almost wishing they *would* interfere. It would provide an excuse to get rid of some of them, an act that would be unwise, but deeply satisfying!

The thought made the spy chuckle all the way to the launch site.

Euterpe's rocket could be reached by one of two paths: the trapdoor at the bottom of the missile silo, or the door that opened onto the narrow catwalk Ramon Korbuscek had traversed earlier that night. Anyone who wanted to tamper with the rocket had to come in by one way or the other.

The A.I. Gang, unaware that Korbuscek had already entered the rocket, was covering both routes.

Wendy represented the first line of defense. She was huddled beneath the metal stairs that led up to the catwalk or down to the trapdoor. She had been stationed there, not entirely to her pleasure, so she could leave when it was time to help Trip and Ray through the security lines. If Black Glove came while she was still here, she was to attempt to take a photo through the wire grid of the stairs.

Rachel was above her, at the top of the silo, lurking in one of the little control alcoves that flanked the corridor leading to the catwalk. Like Wendy, she carried an infrared camera.

Each of the gang had one of these.

Each was hoping to be the one to snap a photo of Black Glove.

And, secretly, each was dreading the possibility of discovering that the spy was someone they knew and loved.

Ramon Korbuscek wondered vaguely what the device he was installing would do. Not that it mattered very much, as long as he was paid for it.

He made the final connection and checked his watch. A grimace twisted his face. The problem with the robot's shrieking alarm had thrown him off schedule. It was later than he had anticipated.

With no time for safety, he opted for speed. Even as Rachel was taking up her vigil, Korbuscek was clambering swiftly and silently down the metal ladder that led to the bottom of the silo.

While Rachel missed the spy, her twin did not. Roger was coming up through the trapdoor just as Korbuscek reached the bottom of the silo.

"Hey!" cried Roger. "What are you doing here?"

Hap, hearing Roger's surprise, scrambled through the trapdoor and was standing beside him almost instantly.

Before either of them could make another move, Korbuscek snapped open the tiny capsule he reserved for such emergencies. Instantly a potent sleeping gas filled the concrete-walled area.

Hap and Roger hit the floor like two sacks of flour dropped from an upstairs window.

Without an instant of hesitation Korbuscek pulled a length of thin but incredibly powerful polyester twine from his pocket. He bound the boys together, hands behind their backs, and pushed them under the rocket.

The spy actually began to whistle as he made his way back to his assigned patrol. Once the rocket was launched and he could report that the device he had installed in the robot had made it into space, he would have more money than he would know what to do with.

And the only two people who could identify him would not only be dead—they would have been completely vaporized!

Rachel toyed restlessly with her pennywhistle, which she had put in the pocket of her coveralls just in case she had a time to practice. But she dared not play it now, of course, for fear of giving away her position should Black Glove come along.

Suddenly the question that had been nagging at the back of her mind since she first took her position forced its way into her consciousness. Though she kept trying to force it aside, it insisted on being paid attention to.

What if Black Glove has already tampered with the rocket?

The gang had been banking on the assumption that spy work of that sort would, of necessity, take place in the dead of the night. But whoever Black Glove really was, his or her other identity was as a respected member of the Anza-bora Island community—a person who might be able to get access to almost anyplace without raising too much suspicion.

Rachel tried to suppress the idea.

It wouldn't go away.

Finally she decided the only thing to do was check the rocket and make sure.

Poking her head around the edge of the alcove where she had been hiding, she looked down the corridor. No sound. No glimmer of light. No other sign of anyone approaching.

Flicking on her flashlight, she stepped onto the catwalk that led to the rocket. *I hope this doesn't upset Hap and Roger,* she thought. *If they see my light, they may think it's Black Glove.*

Of course, even if they did think that, they weren't supposed to do anything—any more than she was if the spy had walked past her. The plan was to snap a picture, not get involved in a fight.

She had no way of knowing the boys could not see her light because bound and gagged, they were lying unconscious beneath the rocket's exhaust vents.

She picked her way carefully along the catwalk. Her light, shining through the gridwork, made eerie shadows against the wall of the missile silo.

When she reached the rocket and could brace herself against it, she looked down. At the sight of that silver tube stretching into the darkness she shivered. The raw power of what they had created still astonished her.

Pressing the same sequence of panels that Korbuscek had earlier in the evening, she opened the door to Euterpe's chamber and peered in. The robot was playing the music of the spheres, the colorful lights on its chest flashing in merry patterns.

"Hi, Twerpy," whispered Rachel. She flashed her light around the chamber. Everything looked fine. But there were a lot of places here to hide a transmitter— even inside Euterpe itself, if you were clever enough.

Deciding she had better check things more carefully, Rachel climbed into the chamber. A number of carefully worded questions aimed at various project scientists had convinced the gang that the smallest device Black Glove could use would have to be at least the size of a standard paperback book.

Rachel had helped design the main chamber. Working with Dr. Weiskopf, she had positioned Euterpe in the center of it. She knew virtually every inch of the space, including every place large enough to hold a device of the size Black Glove might plant. If it was already here, she would find it.

A sound outside the rocket sent a sudden chill shivering down her spine. *What was that?*

Holding her breath, she listened carefully.

Nothing.

She began inching her way around Euterpe, back toward the door.

At the same instant Black Glove stepped into the rocket.

At the sound Rachel swung her flashlight upward. A well-aimed kick from Black Glove sent it flying out of her hand. It bounced off the wall, clattered to the floor, slid under Euterpe. In the jagged movement of the light, Rachel saw two things: her attacker had jet black hair, and wore a pair of smooth black gloves.

A rush of panic rose in her throat. She was about to scream when Black Glove grabbed her.

Instinct overwhelmed fear. She fought as best she could in the tiny space, scratching, kicking, screaming.

But a sudden blow to the head sent her spinning into unconsciousness.

Panting, heart pounding, Black Glove took several deep breaths, then turned to the task of installing the transmitter. The spy could barely suppress the surge of excitement. As soon as the rocket was launched, every bit of top-secret information about Project Alpha could finally be sent to G.H.O.S.T.

Black Glove glanced back at the figure slumped on the floor and felt a twinge of regret. Too bad it had to be Rachel; in many ways, she seemed the most sensible kid in the group. But it was time to teach the brats a lesson they would never forget.

And it had to be done, for as unlikely as it was that she had been able to see her assailant in the dim shreds of colored light that had twinkled on the far side of the robot during their brief fight, it was not an acceptable chance.

She had to go.

Stepping out of the rocket, Black Glove sealed the door shut, thinking, *Space is probably as good a place as any to get rid of a nosy kid.*

19

Rude Awakenings

"I WISH OUR PARENTS WEREN'T SO PROTECTIVE," MUTtered Ray bitterly.

He and Trip were crouched at the edge of the airfield, waiting for Wendy just as their friends had earlier that evening.

Trip nodded. It was embarrassing to be forced to arrive so much later than the rest of the gang.

The Wonderchild showed up a few moments later. Her job this time was more to act as guide than to control the guard robots, since either of the boys could probably have managed that on their own.

"What time is it?" asked Ray.

Trip checked his watch, which brought his wrist about level with Ray and Wendy's heads. "Nearly four. Just three short hours until blastoff." He glanced down at his friends. "That *wasn't* a short joke!" he protested, catching the expression on Wendy's face.

"I didn't say anything!" she exclaimed. "What makes you think I'm so sensitive anyway? To tell you the truth, if I could get something to eat right now, I might even let you tell a short joke and live. I'm starved!"

"I almost forgot!" cried Ray. Digging into his coveralls, he produced a still-warm burger, slathered with everything he had been able to get his hands on. "We brought this for you."

"I can't remember if I was holding anything against you, Ray," Wendy said, just before sinking her teeth into the burger. "If I was, all is forgiven."

When she had finished chewing, or at least nearly so, she outlined their plans: "The main spots are already covered. Hap and Roger are at the base of the rocket, and Rachel is guarding the catwalk. I guess it's more important for us to be available if anything comes up than to guard any specific spot right now."

Trip scuffed at the floor as they began walking through the tunnel. If only his parents hadn't been so strict lately! He felt completely left out. "What time are they going to meet us?" he asked morosely.

"Well, the computer is set to seal everything at six-thirty," said Wendy. She recalled the fast talking they had had to do to arrange that little bit of timing. They had been afraid that if *all* operations had been sealed the night before, as Dr. Weiskopf had wanted, they would lose any chance of catching Black Glove in action.

"Which means we should meet the others at quarter

of seven to watch the launch together," concluded Ray. "Just as planned."

"I know, I know," said Trip. He kicked the wall. "This is going to be one boring night. I wish I was in Hap's shoes right now."

Hap's shoes were actually one of the last places in the world anyone would have wanted to be right then—though at the moment the owner of those shoes was hardly awake enough to be aware of that fact.

As the gas began to wear off, Hap kept *trying* to wake up. But he didn't seem to be able to manage to do it until a groan from Roger, who was lying beside him, penetrated the fog that seemed to cover his brain.

Morning already? he thought. He tried to stretch, but couldn't move his arms. Opening one eye, he found himself staring at the floor.

What was going on here?

"Hap?" moaned a groggy voice next to him. "Are you awake?"

"Roger? Is that you? What are you doing in my bedroom?"

Roger knew he wasn't in Hap's bedroom. But his brain hadn't come into sharp enough focus to figure out where he really was. He squeezed his eyes shut, then opened them again. The view didn't change. He was staring at concrete.

Where's the rug? he wondered. *There ought to be a rug.*

Twisting sideways, Roger looked up and saw a glowing clock face several feet above him. It was the only source of light in the room. The large green numbers said 4:02:37.

Memory began to trickle though the haze in his brain. When it connected with the reality of the clock, the horrible truth came crashing in on him. That was the launch clock! In two hours, fifty-seven minutes, and twenty-three seconds, the rocket was going to blast off!

He lurched sideways again, dragging Hap with him.

"Hey!" cried Hap, roused by the sudden pull against his bonds.

Roger ignored his friend. His throat closed with horror as he found himself staring at the most frightening thing he had ever seen in his life: a set of conical openings that he himself had designed—openings that in less than three hours would erupt with a burst of chemical flame that would sear away first his clothes, then his flesh, and finally his bones themselves.

"Hap," he whispered urgently. "Oh, Hap, we've really done it this time!"

Hap Swenson, fully awake now, stared at the launch clock as it counted down the remaining minutes of his life.

He thought, inevitably, of the time he and Trip had been trapped in what seemed sure to be a watery grave at the island power plant.

They had gotten out then. He and Roger would get out now.

Somehow.

They had to.

Now if only he could convince himself that that was true.

"Keep trying!" hissed Roger. "There's got to be some way out of these ropes!"

"If there is, squirming isn't it."

"Have you got a better idea?"

"Yeah!" said Hap suddenly. "Fins!"

After a moment of wondering if his friend had lost his mind, Roger understood. The base of Euterpe's rocket sported three large fins designed to stabilize the initial stage of its flight. Their edges were hardly razor sharp.

But they might be sharp enough.

"Hap, you're a genius!"

Working together, the boys slid across the floor to one of the fins. Then they maneuvered themselves into a sitting position, banging their shoulders and wrenching their arms in the process.

"Slide to your left a little," said Roger. "I think that will give us more contact."

A moment later they began rubbing their wrists up and down the fin, trying to press the material that bound them against its edge. The edge was dull, but abrasive enough to wear through the cord eventually—if it didn't wear *them* down first. Korbuscek had bound them so tightly that as they slid their hands up and down, the friction was slowly tearing away the skin on their wrists. Blood was already flowing freely down their palms.

"Roger," said Hap after they had worked in silence for several minutes.

"Yeah?"

"What are we going to do if we don't manage to get loose until the silo has been sealed?"

"I'm working on that!" said Roger. He paused. "But be sure to let me know if you get any more brilliant ideas."

He glanced up at the clock. Five-thirty. An hour and a half until launch time.

About forty feet above the boys, Rachel was starting to regain consciousness too. Slowly, trying not to move too fast, she lifted her fingers to her forehead to find out why it hurt so much. To her surprise, she felt an enormous lump.

She opened her eyes. A flickering, colorful glow illuminated her surroundings. Beautiful music washed over her.

She tried to sit up but found she couldn't. She seemed to be blocked from moving in almost every direction.

A lump began building in her chest as panic overtook her.

Suddenly she recognized the music. It was Euterpe's singing! Instantly everything came flooding back to her: Black Glove, the fight, the rocket. . . .

The rocket! She was still in the rocket!

She tried to get to her feet, hurt herself in about five different places, tried again, more carefully.

Moving slowly, she slid one arm underneath her. Then she got a leg free enough to use as a brace. The other was caught in something. Turning her head, she realized that it was held by Euterpe.

A little this way, she thought. *Then if I scooch to the right. . . .*

It was no good. She was still caught.

"Euterpe!" she yelled. "Stop singing and help me!"

That was pointless, of course. The robot didn't respond to that kind of command.

She looked at the door. Euterpe's lights provided just enough illumination for her to realize that Black Glove had sealed it shut. So the message on Wendy's terminal had been true after all. Their enemy *was* desperate enough to kill.

And from the looks of things, she was first in line.

She redoubled her efforts to free her leg.

When it would not come loose, she began to scream.

The spell of panic was brief but terrible. When the frenzy had passed, Rachel put her hands against Euterpe and tried to steady herself. Now that the panic had passed, her mind was clear enough to know that if she was to escape this death trap she would have to use her brains, not her emotions.

She reviewed the plans and functions of the rocket in her mind. Because it was not designed to carry a human, there was no standard radio in the chamber—only a transmitter linked directly to Euterpe, designed to carry its music back to the receivers on Anzabora Island.

The robot continued to sing its cosmic song, completely oblivious to Rachel's danger.

Crunched between the robot and the wall of the rocket, Rachel stared at her watch, willing it to stop, and stop time with it.

An hour and a quarter and it would be all over. The computer would follow the commands locked into its memory a half a day earlier. The top of the silo would swing up. The ignition would be triggered. The mighty thrust engines would roar into life. And Rachel would join Euterpe on its voyage into space.

Unless she could somehow get a message to the outside world.

Unless . . . unless . . .

Rachel sat bolt upright, bumping her head against the robot.

The idea was ridiculous.

But it just might work!

"Euterpe," she said, taking out her pennywhistle. "Get ready to do your thing!"

20

Variations on a Theme

DR. ANTHONY PHILLIPS GROPED HIS WAY OUT OF THE sheets and lay without moving for a moment. Suddenly he sat straight up.

Launch morning!

The twins would never forgive him if he missed it. Throwing aside the sheets, he sprang out of bed. He pushed a button at the side of the bathroom sink that would start the coffee brewing in the kitchen, then stepped into the shower.

Dr. Phillips yawned as he began to work the shampoo into his thinning auburn hair. He felt as if he'd hardly slept at all. These late nights were beginning to get to him.

He dashed out of the shower, dried, dressed, and downed a cup of coffee, then sped to the launch site.

Dr. Fontana was the first person he saw when the guards let him into the observation room. He allowed himself a slight frown. Though he had never been able to put a finger on it, something about the woman bothered him.

She gave him a curt nod, then turned back to the window—a twelve-inch-thick, lead-impregnated piece of glass that would allow them to view the launch close up without being roasted.

The Gammands came in soon after, somehow managing to avoid looking ridiculous when they walked arm in arm, even though Hugh Gammand was nearly two feet taller than his wife.

Dr. Phillips squinted at them, trying to figure out what Hugh was up to. The towering scientist hissed something that sounded like "Down, Thugwad!" then smacked his pocket several times.

Dr. Phillips shrugged. Gammand had always been a trifle eccentric.

The room was filling rapidly now. He wondered when his children would arrive.

Probably performing some last-minute checks, he thought, chuckling to himself. *You'd think this was a manual operation, instead of being completely computerized!*

Suddenly the observation room was flooded with beautiful music.

He glanced at his watch. Six-thirty. They might as well forget it. They couldn't change anything now without going through the main computer.

*   *   *

182

Roger leaned his head against the fin and tried to will the pain in his wrists out of existence. His hands were slippery with blood, and the bonds didn't seem any closer to separating than they had an hour ago. *What are these damn things made of?* he wondered desperately.

Suddenly he heard a muted clanging sound above him.

He groaned. It was the door from the catwalk into the corridor; the computer had just sealed off their last possible avenue of escape.

"That's it," he said wearily. "There's no point in going on. It won't make any difference even if we do break loose."

Hap's voice when he responded was close to a growl. "Roger, if I go, I plan to go fighting. So stop moaning and get back to work!"

Roger smiled. Other than the fact that he didn't want his friend to die, he couldn't think of anyone better to share a spot like this with than Hap Swenson. "Okay, boss," he said. "Back to work it is."

"Good," said Hap. He glanced up at the clock. "We've got twenty-five minutes and thirty-six seconds left to live. Let's make the most of them.

"All right, Twerpy," said Rachel. "I got them to build this rocket for you. Now it's your turn to come through for me!"

She pushed a little switch on the robot's neck. "Ready?" she asked, not caring that she was talking to something that couldn't understand a word she said. She stared at her pennywhistle for a moment, then raised it to her lips.

But she didn't play. Lowering the whistle, she dried her sweaty palms on her coveralls and thought, *Oh, muse of music, if you're still around anywhere, I sure need you now. Please—let me get the pitch right just this once!*

Euterpe's lights had stopped blinking; the robot sat quietly, waiting for new input.

Rachel put the whistle to her lips.

The first note was terrible—a squawk that would have offended Euterpe's ears, if a robot was capable of being offended.

Rachel licked her lips and tried again.

Better, but still no response from Euterpe.

One more try. This time she produced a single pure note.

Euterpe repeated it.

Rachel drew a deep breath and let it out in relief. "All right, Euterpe," she said. "It's time to jam!"

She began playing the simple nine-note phrase she hoped would save her life. *Don't get too fancy with this, Twerpy,* she thought. *The message won't do any good if no one understands it!*

Trip, Ray, and Wendy spent the last hours before daylight in a previously chosen supply room, waiting for the others to join them.

"So where are they?" asked Trip angrily, a little

before seven. "It's not enough they got to have all the fun last night. Do they have to leave us sitting here now?"

"Calm down," said Wendy, stifling a yawn. "You're starting to sound like me!"

"Maybe we missed them," said Ray. "They might have been running late and gone to the observation room by some other route."

"That's probably it," said Wendy, heaving herself to her feet. "I bet they're waiting there now. Let's go!"

She began trotting along the hallway.

"I wonder if they got a picture of Black Glove," said Trip, rising to join her. "I bet she was here last night!"

"You don't think something might have happened to them, do you?" asked Ray.

"Not all three of them," said Wendy. "If it was just one, I'd be worried. But I can't see B.G. taking out all three of them."

"I suppose you're right," said Ray. "Hey, listen— they've turned on Euterpe!"

"You mean they turned on the sound system," said Trip. "Euterpe's been running her music since we put her in there."

"Jeez, get technical, why don't you?" muttered Ray.

Wendy stopped. "That doesn't sound like the music of the spheres to me."

Ray shrugged. "So Jupiter is farther away than the last time you heard it. The song changes all the time, remember?"

"Of course. But this is something different." She pressed her hands against her forehead. "I know that rhythm. What is it? *What is it?*"

Trip and Ray glanced at each other and shrugged. Wendy tended to get like this sometimes.

Roger was having a hard time keeping his eyes off the clock: 6:51:22 it read now. Less than nine minutes to go before the burst of all-consuming fire.

He almost wished the time would move even faster, bring this tortured waiting to an end.

Hap refused to look at the clock. "Keep working!" he snapped when he felt Roger begin to slow down.

"Why?" asked Roger wearily.

But he resumed rubbing his bonds against the rocket's fin.

Rachel, too, was checking the time.

Six minutes until liftoff.

She had lost track of how many times she had played her message. There had been no response.

What's the matter with you people? she though desperately. *Are you deaf? Can't you understand?*

Of course, it would help if Euterpe would just repeat her notes instead of turning the simple rhythm into a small corner of variations on her theme.

Rachel set down the whistle and laid her head against Euterpe. No need to play any longer. The robot would continue creating variations without her input for several minutes—probably until the moment of liftoff.

Though she tried to suppress the image, she could not help imagining the moment, the press of gravity as she began a trip into space from which she would never return. Her spirit finally broke. Leaning her head against Euterpe's hard metallic body, she began to weep.

Wendy, Ray, and Trip emerged from one of the smaller buildings onto the airfield.

Euterpe's music was being broadcast through the huge speakers mounted at the ends of the field. Somehow the atmosphere reminded them of a holiday, or a fair.

Suddenly Wendy grabbed Trip's arm. "I've got it!" she cried. *"I've got it!"* She clutched his sleeve even tighter. "Don't you hear it?"

"Hear what?" asked Trip, mystified.

"What Euterpe is playing!"

Trip sighed. "Yeah, it's the music of the—"

"It's *not* the music of the spheres!" she yelled. *"Listen!* She's going up and down, all over the place with them, just like when she jams with Dr. Weiskopf. She's playing variations on a theme. One theme, over and over. One nine-note theme. Three short notes, three long notes, three short notes."

"My God!" cried Ray. "It's an SOS!"

"You got it, baby," said the Wonderchild. "Someone is stuck inside that rocket!"

*   *   *

From his assigned patrol route Ramon Korbuscek heard the strange music being broadcast from the rocket. Without actually translating it, he knew at once that something was wrong.

His senses instantly became more alert. A cold sweat broke out on his chest. If anything should interfere with the launch, he had to make sure the device he had planted in the rocket could not be found.

He knew enough about the way the launch was set up to expect it to proceed as scheduled, since it would be almost impossible to abort the mission at this point. But on the off chance that something did happen, he wanted to position himself to be first to reach the rocket.

Looking around to make sure he was not being observed, he sprinted toward the closest tunnel that could lead him to the missile silo.

"Where's the nearest computer that connects to the main terminal?" asked Trip.

"The control room," said Wendy. "I saw one when I was in there last night."

"Well, let's move!" yelled Ray.

Starting a dash across the airfield, the three friends came face-to-face with a pair of Sergeant Brody's guards, one male, one female.

"Where do you kids think you're going?" asked the woman. "You should be under cover by now!"

"Take us to the control tower," said Wendy, clambering into their Jeep.

"No can do, Short Stuff," said the guard. "The building is sealed until after the launch."

"But it's *our* launch!" said Wendy.

The guard shrugged. "Orders are orders."

"This is a matter of life and death!" cried Ray.

The woman smiled. "Yeah, it always is with you kids. Why aren't you in the observation room where you can get a close-up look? I would think—hey, get back here!"

The kids were running as fast as they could for the nearest building. The guards started after them.

"We'll have to split up!" cried Trip.

Wendy and Ray peeled off in opposite directions.

The two guards, faced with chasing kids headed in three directions, opted to aim for Trip and Ray.

"I hate it when a woman is a male chauvinist," muttered Wendy. Pulling the robot control device from her pocket, she twisted a dial and pressed a series of buttons.

An instant later every security robot within a thousand yards was rolling in her direction.

21

The Robot Brigade

"THREE MINUTES AND FIFTEEN SECONDS," SAID HAP.

"Will you stop that!" cried Roger. "I don't need an announcer to let me know when I'm going to fry!"

"I'm just trying to motivate you."

"I'm plenty motivated! The damn thing won't cut!"

"Well, lean into it!" said Hap, dragging his weight against the fin as he continued to saw at the cords holding him to Roger.

To his amazement, they separated with a sudden snap that dropped both of them to the floor.

"We did it!" cried Roger, starting to laugh. "Hap, we did it!"

"You bet we did!" said Hap, rubbing his wrists. "Now start working on your feet."

"Here," said Roger, handing him the knife he had just pulled from the pocket of his coveralls. "It's faster."

Hap smiled as he took the knife and sliced through the cords. Then he glanced at the steel ladder that led to the top of the silo. "What do you think would happen if we climbed up to the catwalk?"

Roger shrugged. "It might mean there would be something left of us to bury."

"Well, let's go! At this stage of the game, every little bit counts."

The observation room was in an uproar.

"Something is going on out there!" cried Trip's father. "And I want to know what it is!"

"Abort the launch!" cried several people. "Stop it now!"

Dr. Hwa was trying to calm the group. "There is no way to stop it," he said over and over.

Staff Sergeant Brody looked out the window and groaned. He had suspected this whole thing would be a pain in the neck from the moment two months ago when he first heard the kids were planning to launch a rocket. But even his wildest nightmares had not prepared him for what he saw now: a virtual herd of his security robots racing across the airfield at top speed, with that wretched Wendy Wendell *riding* on the shoulders of the one in the lead!

"Come on, Deathmonger!" cried Wendy, kicking the robot as if it were a balky horse. "Come on, we don't have all day!"

"What we've got is about two and a half minutes!" cried Trip, who was straddling the shoulders of the robot on Wendy's right.

"How long will it take to get into the system?" asked Wendy.

"About ninety seconds!" yelled Ray, who was riding the robot to her left.

"Then we'll just have to move a little faster!" cried the Wonderchild. Reaching into her coveralls, she pulled out the control pack and punched a sequence of buttons. She barely had time to grab Deathmonger's neck before the robot shot forward so fast it nearly sent her flying. Her cap blew off, leaving her pigtails to flap in the wind.

The control tower loomed ahead of them.

"How long?" asked Wendy.

"Two minutes, three seconds," said Trip.

Ignoring her own hatless state, she cried, "Then hold on to your hats! We've got to force the door!"

The robot brigade hurtled forward, then crashed into the solid metal of the doors. They didn't give immediately, but the robots continued to crush in from the rear.

The doors began to bulge.

Seconds later they sprang apart. The robots surged through like water through a bursting dam.

"Come on!" cried Trip, scrambling off his "steed" and sprinting down the hallway. "No time to waste!"

His long legs pumping like pistons, he took the stairs three and four at a bound. No time now to worry about offending his shorter friends. . . .

* * *

"Do you suppose we could grab the top of the silo when it opens for the launch?" asked Hap.

Roger shook his head. "The flaps are too far away. Even if we stood on the nose of the rocket—which I doubt we could do—we couldn't reach them."

The boys were halfway up the side of the silo, clinging to the steel ladder. Another few rungs brought Roger face-to-face with the launch clock.

"Two minutes, fifteen seconds," he said. "Hap, it's been a privilege."

"The pleasure was all mine, buddy. Now here's another idea. What if we climb onto the rocket and try to jump off just as it's lifting out of the silo?"

Roger laughed. "That is the craziest idea I ever heard in my life."

"Do you have a better one?"

"No."

"Then let's try it."

Roger took a last look down at the base of the rocket. In less than ninety seconds the missile silo would be a raging inferno.

Suddenly Hap's idea didn't seem quite so crazy.

Rachel lifted the whistle to her lips and began to play again. If no one had decoded her message by now, it wouldn't make any difference what Euterpe broadcast.

She played a song Dr. Weiskopf had taught her, a beautiful but mournful ballad lamenting life's short sweetness. As she played, she felt a strange sense of peace filter through her.

Euterpe picked up the tune, playing counterpoint to the simple melody.

I just wish we'd put in a window, thought Rachel as she ran her fingers over the whistle's holes. *Euterpe doesn't need one, of course. But if I'm going to die in space, I sure would love to get a chance to enjoy the view before I go.*

Trip Davis stood at the keyboard, trying to keep his fingers from trembling.

"Sherlock" he typed, trying to call up their secret program.

The screen flashed green. Then a question mark appeared.

Trip typed in his personal code, cursed as he realized he had misspelled it, and tried again.

The clock on the wall gave him seventy seconds.

The doors on the top of the missile silo, visible from where he stood, were beginning to open. The sight jolted him into hitting another wrong key. He cried out in anguish. He was going to kill his friends with typing errors!

Taking a breath, he forced himself to slow down. Then he typed in the code word correctly.

The terminal lacked a voice synthesizer. The response appeared on the small screen: "Good morning, Trip. How are you today?"

Trip began typing in the commands that would abort the launch.

"Forty-five seconds!" cried Ray, rushing up behind him.

Trip jumped and typed the wrong character. "Be quiet!" he screamed.

Wendy, barreling into the room right behind Ray, had all she could do to keep from pushing her tall friend away from the keyboard.

Trip felt the sweat pouring down his brow. There. That was it!

He pushed the entry key.

For an agonizing moment, nothing happened.

"Ten," said Ray, counting down with the clock on the wall. "Nine, eight, seven—"

A siren began to wail.

Mission aborted! flashed the screen. *Mission aborted!*

Trip sank to his knees in front of the keyboard.

Across the airfield, the reaction to the siren was instant and almost unanimous.

Rachel, unable to believe it at first, threw her arms around Euterpe. "We're safe!" she cried ecstatically.

Hap and Roger, clinging to the side of the rocket and bracing themselves for the thrust of launch, looked at each other and began to whoop with delight.

The adults in the observation tower, who were close enough to the silo actually to see Hap and Roger clinging to the rocket's smooth metal sides when the launch doors had opened, broke into wild cheers.

But for one of those adults it was a false joy, masking a ferocious rage. Smiling and cheering with the others, inside Black Glove was thinking: *I can't believe they've done it again. What does it take to stop those kids?*

One other adult was not happy. Ramon Korbuscek, desperate to retrieve the device he had planted inside Euterpe, threw open the door to the missile silo and stepped out onto the catwalk. He stopped in shock when he saw Roger climbing down from the side of the rocket.

What is he doing up here? I can't have any witnesses now. None!

Unaware that he could be seen from the observation room, and unable to see Hap from where he stood, Korbuscek flung himself at Roger. Even now it shouldn't be too difficult to explain one body lying at the base of the rocket. A simple slip in the dark could have caused it.

Roger, backing down from the rocket and thinking he was safe at last, let out a bellow of fear when someone's arms wrapped around his chest and muscled him toward the edge of the catwalk.

"Hey, let go of him!" cried Hap, coming around the edge of the rocket.

Another one! Fueled by desperation, Korbuscek wrenched Roger closer to the edge.

He had nearly pushed him over when the redhead grabbed the catwalk's iron rail. But Roger's bloodied palms began to slip as Korbuscek pulled at his arms.

Only the adrenaline charging through his body gave him enough strength to cling to the railing until Hap made it onto the catwalk. The husky blond launched himself at the raging spy, distracting his attention from Roger.

Still holding Roger with one arm, Korbuscek lashed out at Hap, landing a backhanded punch that sent him to his knees, then slipping over the edge of the catwalk.

Mrs. Swenson, watching from the observation tower, screamed and grabbed her husband's arm—even as her son grabbed the edge of the catwalk just in time to avoid plunging to the bottom of the silo.

With the top open and the morning sun flooding in, the bottom of that pit was easily visible. Dangling from the catwalk, Hap looked past his feet and felt his stomach lurch.

Korbuscek yanked at Roger, trying to break his grip on the railing. At the same time he tried to maneuver himself into position to stamp on Hap's fingers.

His hands slick with his own blood, Hap was having a hard time clinging to the metal catwalk. When Korbuscek's boot slammed against the railing just a fraction of an inch from his fingers, it took everything he had to keep from flinching away—a flinch that would have sent him hurtling to the bottom of the shaft.

The observation room had erupted into chaos. The adults were screaming for action. Most were rushing for the door, getting in each other's way as they scrambled to try to get to the endangered boys.

Anthony Phillips, however, was pressed against the

observation window. He knew there was no way to get to the silo to help his son. All he could do was watch and ache, as a madman tried to murder his child. His long-standing belief in psychic powers dropped aside as he tried to send his own strength across the gap to Roger.

Hold on, son, he thought desperately. *Hold on!*

It was Dr. Remov who ended things. Shouldering his way to the front of the room, he shoved Brody away from the control panel the sergeant was using to communicate with his men, then picked up the microphone. He turned to stare at the battle. He watched intently, waiting for the right moment—the moment that would cause the boys the least jeopardy.

Hap had managed to get one leg back on the catwalk and was trying to climb up again.

Korbuscek spotted him and aimed a ferocious kick at his head.

Now! thought Remov when he spotted the spy raising his foot. *Now, while he's off balance!*

Flicking on the microphone, he spoke a single word.

Though his authoritative voice was quiet, the word—a word he had embedded in Ramon Korbuscek's subconscious mind years before—did its work.

Overwhelmed by a wave of panic, the spy leaped away from the boys he was trying to kill, and fell to his death.

Epilogue

A few nights after a second attempt at a launch had gone off without a hitch, the A.I. Gang relaxed in front of a small campfire on the north beach of Anzabora Island.

Rachel looked around. It felt good to have all of them here together—even Wendy, who had broken the long-standing tension that had simmered between them when she asked meekly if saving Rachel's skin might not be accepted in lieu of a long overdue apology.

Now the Wonderchild was acting as referee while Trip and Roger wrestled on the sand. Not far away Ray was sitting on his basketball, toasting a marshmallow.

Rachel leaned back. "Look," she said, pointing up.

Hap Swenson followed the line of her finger. "What?" he asked.

Darkness was falling, the stars slowly coming out of hiding.

Rachel shrugged. "Euterpe's up there somewhere," she said. "Not quite so far away as all those stars. But she's definitely there. She's part of the heavens now, like she was meant to be."

She settled back on her elbows, her fiery-red hair brushing against he sand. It made her feel good to think of Euterpe circling the earth, singing her cosmic melody.

The fire crackled. The ocean surged against the shore.

Rachel smiled. Even the fact that the transmitter discovered during the search of the rocket had been blamed on Ramon Korbuscek—leaving the gang with no more tangible proof of Black Glove's existence than before—was not enough to mar her mood tonight.

What she didn't know, what none of them knew yet, was that the robot they had set to circling the planet still carried within it the device *actually* installed by Ramon Korbuscek—a device that carried the power to plunge the world into a nuclear nightmare.

They didn't know that now.

But it wouldn't be long before they found out.

About the Author

BRUCE COVILLE was born in Syracuse, New York. He grew up in a rural area north of the city, around the corner from his grandparents' dairy farm. In the years before he was able to make his living full time as a writer Bruce was, among other things, a gravedigger, a toymaker, a magazine editor, and a door-to-door salesman. He loves reading, musical theater, and being outdoors.

In addition to his nearly fifty books for young readers, Bruce has written poems, plays, short stories, newspaper articles, thousands of letters, and several years' worth of journal entries.

He lives in a brick house in Syracuse with his wife, his youngest child, three cats, and a dog named Booger. The dog's name was not his idea.

Some of Bruce's best-known books are *My Teacher Is an Alien; Goblins in the Castle;* and *Aliens Ate My Homework.*